THE HONEY FIELD

laura boggess

the poetry club series

𝑡𝑠 T. S. Poetry Press • New York

T. S. Poetry Press
New York
Tspoetry.com

Cover image by Sora Sagano, Creative Commons, Unsplash
https://unsplash.com/@sorasagano

ISBN 978-1-943120-72-7

Cataloging-in-Publication Data:
Boggess, Laura
        [Fiction.]
        The Honey Field.
            The poetry club series/Laura Boggess
        ISBN 978-1-943120-72-7

1

No one had checked on the bees since early spring—not since Corrie got sick. She'd been meaning to get down there for weeks, but there was the funeral, and then the estate to settle …the sympathy cards to acknowledge…the food and flowers. All summer long the bees had been left to tend to themselves. To which, Corrie had said, *don't worry about it. Those bees know better than we do how to do the work they do. Just make sure there's no robbing going on. And check the queens. Make sure the hives are all still queenright.*

The morning sun was mild, so she pulled on her garden boots and walked down the hill to the apiary. She wasn't planning on opening the boxes. Not yet. She'd wait until the afternoon when they would be out foraging. But the thought of the neglected hives had been nagging on her all week. She just wanted to look them over from the outside, see if there was anything obvious amiss. Besides, she needed to brush up on the inspection technique. She'd never done this by herself. Corrie kept all the equipment and the protective gear in a shed close to the hives. She'd just look around. Scare off the snakes. Re-familiarize herself with all the things.

In truth, she'd never wanted the blasted critters. But she could never say no to Corrie. Whatever Corrie wanted; Corrie got. Ever since they were kids. There never was anybody but Corrie for her. They'd both had false starts. But it didn't take long for them to find their way back to one another. And now, here she was, 25 years later. Left to deal with the infernal bees on her own.

How it would grieve Corrie if she were to lose these bees.

It took a few minutes before she realized she was crying. Angrily, she wiped her eyes with the back of her hand. She was so tired of crying.

Do not stand at my grave and weep.

She'd read it just this morning. That poem by Mary Elizabeth Frye. It was in a collection of poems someone sent in the mail by way of condolences. What was that book called? *Earth Song.* That was it. "A Nature Poems Experience," read the subtitle. Who sent that book? Ah, yes. It was Sarah. Corrie's only daughter. Sarah knew. "May these words heal your heart the way they are healing mine. May you find peace and solace in nature and the many memories you shared surrounded by this good earth."

She remembered the words easily because they reminded her of Corrie so much.

> *Do not stand at my grave and weep.*
> *I am not there. I do not sleep.*
> *I am a thousand winds that blow.*
> *I am the diamond glints on snow.*
>
> *I am the sunlight on ripened grain.*
> *I am the gentle autumn rain.*
> *When you awaken in the morning's hush*
> *I am the swift uplifting rush*
>
> *Of quiet birds in circled flight.*

I am the soft stars that shine at night.
Do not stand at my grave and cry;
I am not there. I did not die.

Corrie had said something of the like before passing.

"Don't cry when I'm gone. I can't abide the thought of you crying. Not for me. Not for anything. Just remember how happy we've been. How many good years we've had. Remember that first time I kissed you—under the stars, out in the meadow. Remember how surprised we both were. And how many kisses we've had since. Remember that. It will make you smile, like it's making me smile right now."

It did make her smile. Through tears, sure, but she was smiling.

The shed was being overtaken by multiflora rose. Darn that stuff! She recalled Corrie's battles with the invasive shrub and shook her head in frustration. She'd have to get the Brown boys out here to do some weed eating. They'd done a nice job on the front lawn. She wasn't one for lawn maintenance. She'd do just about anything but.

She sighed and approached the shed, stomping heavily to warn any snakes in the vicinity. The door only stuck a little, swollen with rain and neglect. She shouldered her way in, wiping a spider-web from the entry as she passed through.

Inside, it took a minute for her eyes to adjust to the dim light. She inhaled. It smelled of earth and dust. She walked over to one of the windows and lifted the blind to let the morning light in, waving away more cobwebs on the way, then looked around. Everything was tidy and in its proper place, if not in need of a good airing out. A single shaft of sunlight fell through the pane, honeying Corrie's oak potting table, illuminating dust motes in the air. The bee suit hung on a hook on the west wall and the light was slowly moving up the length of it. The years had yellowed the coarse white fabric. The veil sat on the floor at its feet, along with the gloves. Everything was still…waiting.

Earth-scent, golden light, a song in her brain, a memory, a memory, a memory…

Suddenly the beauty of it all was too much and she had to leave.

~

That night she fell asleep reading *Earth Song* and dreamed of "Inversnaid."

"It was inspired by the season Hopkins spent in a village in the Scottish Highlands," Sarah had told her when she asked. "*Burn* is the word for *brook* in the Scottish dialect. He uses some other Scottish dialectic words that can make it a tricky poem to read if you don't know. Google up an analysis of the poem and you'll see what I mean."

She had. And now in the dream she was walking beside a stream in the Scottish Highlands. The dew-soaked hills surrounding her fell into the water, creating a rolling reel of light and shadow, filling her spirit with an indescribable ecstasy...

> *What would the world be, once bereft*
> *Of wet and of wildness? Let them be left,*
> *O let them be left, wildness and wet;*
> *Long live the weeds and the wilderness yet.*

She reached out beside her to grab Corrie's hand…

The tolling tones of her cell phone jarred her awake. It took a minute to re-orient, but the phone kept ringing. She grieved losing a Corrie visitation. These visits were becoming ever rarer. Poetry seemed to bring them on, so she made a mental note to read at least one poem a day from the book. She sighed and picked up the intruding call.

"Hello?"

"Hey, friend, it's Rhoda. Sorry I missed your call. What's up?"

"Hey, there! Thanks for getting back to me so quickly. I have a favor to ask, and please, don't hesitate to say no if you're too busy."

There was a slight pause, so she rushed forth with her request.

"It's Corrie's bees. I was wondering if you'd have time to help me get up to speed on their keeping. They haven't been inspected since late spring, before, ah, before Corrie was too sick to tend to them. I've been down to the meadow and done an outside inspection. Saw nothing alarming, no robbing, no excessive bee carcasses outside, no evidence of critter tampering…I just…Well, when it came to opening the hives, I chickened out. I'm afraid I'll do something wrong."

There was still silence from the other end. Finally, Rhoda said, "Corrie's bees," slowly, as if trying to figure something out.

"Yep," she responded.

"They look good from the outside?"

"Yep."

Another pause.

"I think I can make time to help you inspect. How many hives all together?"

"Just seven. All in proximity."

"Tell you what, if you don't mind me bringing a class down to observe, we could come this Saturday afternoon. Would that work?"

"Yes, of course, that would be wonderful! Thank you, Rhoda. I'm so, so grateful."

"I'll email you specifics of the logistics, but I'll bring my own tools, so there shouldn't be much prep required. This is actually great experience for my student beekeepers. So thanks goes to you."

She felt her eyes begin to smart at her friend's graciousness.

"You're the best, Rhoda."

~

Saturday arrived with blue sky and low humidity. She had gathered all the gear Rhoda suggested and placed it outside the shed for easy access: smoker, hive tool, bee brush, protective gear, a couple of additional boxes and frames in case they needed to add on to the existing setup, and the first aid kit for any emergencies. Though Rhoda would bring supplies, she herself wanted to do some of the hands-on work so she could develop the confidence needed to take care of the bees.

She was nervous. Not about the bees, but the people. She hadn't spoken to one single person, other than Sarah—and the Brown boys—since Corrie's funeral. And she'd only spoken to them on the phone. She knew she'd become a bit of a recluse, but still had little desire for company. Now she was welcoming a group of ten or so people, not only into her meadow, but her home. She'd offered to provide lunch for the group as a way of thanking them for their help and had picked up some cheeses at the deli, some portabella caps to roast, and and thrown together a quick sandwich tray to keep things simple. But Corrie always said she couldn't keep things simple and, true to form, she'd decided last night to make peach tarts to throw in the oven while everyone was eating their sandwiches. The tarts only needed to bake for fifteen minutes, and there was that bushel of peaches the Brown boys brought when they mowed the grass last week. The recipe called for rosemary honey drizzled on top—a perfect pairing with their bee work. There were still several jars of Corrie's honey in the pantry. She decided to put the tarts together ahead of time, hoping the puff pastry wouldn't get gummy, so all she'd have to do is pop them in the oven when the group returned to the house.

The class would be arriving at eleven, so there was an hour to prepare. She pulled the shallots out of the fridge and carefully washed and dried them before cutting them into thin slices. Then she heated some olive oil and sauteed the shallots, stirring in apple cider vinegar after a couple minutes to caramelize it all nicely. Pinch of salt and twist of the pepper mill. Setting that aside, she sliced up the peaches, ignoring the juice oozing over the cutting block. Then she sliced two wheels of brie and pulled out the puff pastry she'd thawed overnight. She cut the pastry into twelve individual portions (to be safe—always better to have more than less when entertaining). Over the individual squares she layered shallots, brie slices, fresh basil (chopped), and the peaches. She folded the edges of the pastry up and pressed the tines of a fork over the lip. Then she brushed egg wash over the edges; she would drizzle a little more oil and add more salt and pepper before putting them in the oven. She'd made the rosemary honey last night (2/3 cup honey, 4 tablespoons chopped fresh rosemary, cracked black pepper to taste) so the flavors had time to mingle.

Sliding the tray of tarts into the fridge, she glanced at the clock. They would be here in twenty minutes! She ran to the bathroom and did a quick swab on the toilet, then ran a comb through her limp hair. She stared at herself in the mirror for a minute, trying to decide if she cared enough to add some lipstick.

She leaned in closer to her reflection. The ten pounds she'd lost in the past three months showed in her face, her eyes and cheeks hollowed out, sinking deeper into her round chin and jawline. There were purple shadows under her eyes, etchings around the beak of her mouth. She looked like an owl—round and angular all at once. What was that line she'd read in the *Earth Song* poems this morning? *The owl rehearses a song to life. It refuses to presage its own death.*

Is that what she was doing? If she rehearsed—pretended —a song of life, would her heart begin to beat again?

She remembered something Corrie had said in the last days.

"Please take care of your body. I know how you forget to eat when you're sad. I know how you stop sleeping. Don't do that when I'm gone, ok? Take care of that body that I love so much. Do it for me. Please?"

She grabbed an elastic and pulled her hair into a ponytail. She wasn't sure it helped but at least it tidied up her appearance. She opened the drawer in the vanity. Her fingers hesitated over a small tube of pink when the doorbell rang.

She closed the drawer quietly. One thing at a time.

2

There were ten of them altogether, including herself. They trudged down the hill in a single line, carrying veils and gloves, Rhoda with a backpack weighed down with her favorite bee-keeping tools. Ever the teacher, she talked over her shoulder as they picked their way through the grasses.

"Why did we wait until well after sunrise to conduct this inspection? Why not do it earlier when it's not so hot?"

A skinny voice piped up from somewhere behind. "You wanted to wait until foraging time. That way we would be less of a disturbance."

Rhoda nodded. "Right. Good. The fewer bees home the better for us all. We need to have a plan before we open the boxes. I want you all to stand back as much as you can and still be able to observe. We'll approach the hives from behind, so as not to alarm the guard bees. Our hostess and I will be the main ones inspecting, but we'll let you handle everything and have a good look if you like. I'll do the first few frames by way of instruction. When we find the queens, I'll signal for you all to come forward, one at a time, to see. Remember to move slowly and calmly. A nervous person makes for nervous bees."

They approached the storage shed and Rhoda put her backpack down.

"We'll light our smokers here and then don our protective gear."

There was a quiet bustling as everyone pulled on veils and gloves. She retrieved her own smoker and the bucket of dried pine needles and cedar shavings Corrie had always used for fuel. She packed her smoker tightly and got a good flame before offering the fuel bucket to Rhoda. She tucked her hive tool and bee brush into the belt she had looped around her waist and felt suddenly surprised how natural it felt to be handling Corrie's instruments. Maybe she hadn't forgotten after all.

She and Rhoda advanced to the first hive, the students lingering behind. Rhoda blew some smoke into the bee door and under the cover. Working quickly, she removed the outer cover and set it on its side, then inserted the edge of her hive tool between the cover and hive box to pop loose the propolis, or bee glue, tacking it down. After that, she lifted the cover just enough to blow a little more smoke under it and set it back down, giving it time to work on the bees inside. Then she set the inner cover aside also, taking care in case there were still some bees still clinging. Next, she began removing the stacked boxes, supers and brood boxes until she got to the bottommost box. The boxes were heavy, and Corrie had placed some cinder blocks nearby to prevent back strain. She helped Rhoda lift, using her hive tool to separate boxes when necessary, and covered the stack of boxes with an old canvas throw Corrie used as a hive manipulation cloth. She knew this was to keep the bees calm and protect them from other intruders. Corrie used to sing to the bees when working their territories. Usually a Billy Joel song. Most of the time it was "Just the Way You Are." Corrie loved Billie Joel. She smiled, remembering.

Now it was time to take a look at the frames. Rhoda used a hive tool to pry the outermost frame away from the others. When able, Rhoda gripped the frame with both hands and pulled it slowly up out of the box, studying the frame closely and gesturing for the others to look. "I don't see any brood in this outer frame, which is good. If there were some brood here, it would mean the bees need more space and we'd have to add a new box." Rhoda gently placed the frame next to the cover and turned her attention to the other frames.

They had decided to look at several frames, enough to re-assure themselves the hive was doing well. They saw new eggs, larvae, and capped brood in all the frames they inspected. When they were most of the way through the box, Rhoda let out an exclamation.

"There's the queen!" She pointed it out for everyone to see and they came, one at a time to get a good look. "She's a beauty!"

They silently watched the larger bee roam around among her subjects for a bit, quieted by the dance. Rhoda looked up at her and smiled.

"Everything looks great in this box. If I'm not mistaken, Corrie anticipated a season of neglect and had everything ready, just in case."

Oh, Corrie.

They replaced all the frames they'd removed exactly as be-fore and began stacking the boxes, inspecting a few frames in each one until they were satisfied all was well.

All seven colonies were inspected in a little under two hours. Rhoda took her time, letting each of the students take a turn to use the various tools, handle the frames, search out the queens. The sun was resting high in the sky when they shed their protective gear.

She found herself humming "Uptown Girl" on the way

up the hill.

~

"You know, I can take those bees off your hands if you like."

They were alone in the kitchen, putting up lunch. The others were in the living room, reviewing what they'd learned, laughing loudly, and comparing cell phone pictures. Before she could respond, their quiet conversation was interrupted.

"Omigosh, these tarts are a-mazing!" She recognized the skinny voice that had spoken up on the way down the hill, mouth now full of tart. "You have to give me this recipe!" This person looked twelve years old. Could she possibly know her way around a kitchen? The girl closed her eyes, leaned against the kitchen doorframe, and savored. "What is that (*chew, chew*) little (*chew*) tang I'm tasting? Ever so subtle, but the perfect touch with the honey and brie." Peach juice was running down her chin, honey dripped from her fingertips.

"You might be tasting the little bit of apple cider I used to deglaze the shallots. I'd be glad to give you the recipe. It's pretty easy to make if you have the right ingredients."

The girl dimpled. "Thank you so much! I'm hosting a bridal shower next week and this would be perfect on the menu. Here, let me give you my card. If you email it to me, that would be great."

A bridal shower! When was the last time…The girl handed her a plain ivory card with the state parks and recreation logo at the top. She scanned the simple print.

Anna Ferris, botanist, naturalist

Division of Natural Resources

"Oh! You're a botanist! You look much too young," she

smiled. "And one of our naturalists too. Corrie was so dedicated to that program. Did you know…"

The words came out before she had a chance to think about them and she regretted them immediately. How could she? Bring up Corrie's name like a bit of small talk? Anna's face changed from one of open pleasure to a mask of sympathy.

"I'm older than I look. I've had my bachelor's for three years. Working on my doctorate now. And, yes, I did—know Corrie. I made a point to take every class Corrie taught in the program. I've never met anyone who understood the natural world so thoroughly! Such a phenomenal teacher … I will always be grateful for …"

"Yes, yes," she said, dropping Anna's card on the table and turning to the sink. "I'll send you the recipe tonight." She turned on the hot water and started piling saucers and coffee cups in to soak. Rhoda studied her face from across the room.

Anna hesitated before joining and helping stack dishes. "I'm sorry. I didn't mean to be insensitive. I just…I am not giving you platitudes. Corrie's passion for the earth is the reason I continued on with the naturalist program. Sometimes a person comes along and changes the way you see the world. Corrie did that for me."

Me too, she thought. She let her hands soak in the hot, sudsy water. Suddenly, she was exhausted. She shifted her gaze out the window into the back yard. There was no wind and the sun languished hazily in the western sky. *We need some rain,* she thought, and sighed heavily.

"Thank you. I'm the one who should apologize. It's still just…very hard for me."

"Of course. I understand."

Anna reached over and squeezed her shoulder awkwardly before leaving the kitchen. Rhoda moved over beside her and joined in, rinsing, and then drying the dishes already washed.

"The bees?" Rhoda asked, wiping the inside of a mug.

She felt her phone vibrate and dried her hands slowly before removing it from her pocket. She stared at the screen blankly for a moment before tapping, "ignore call."

Rhoda exhaled loudly beside her. "Well?"

"Let me think about it," was all she could say because of the sudden lump in her throat.

~

That night, she read more poems and Corrie came to her again.

Corrie never spoke in the dreams, just looked at her with those gray eyes, stayed close by—sometimes taking her hand, sometimes touching her face, sometimes walking just ahead, out of reach. Tonight, she rested her head in Corrie's lap and Corrie combed fingers gently through her hair. The Billy Joel song "Honesty" was playing somewhere in the background. When she woke up, her face was wet with tears.

~

It was this one that sent her into a tailspin of apathy and caused her to take to her bed again:

> On the day when the lotus bloomed, alas, my mind was
>   straying,
> and I knew it not. My basket was empty and the flower

remained unheeded.

Only now and again a sadness fell upon me, and I started up from my

dream and felt a sweet trace of a strange fragrance in the south wind.

The vague sweetness made my heart ache with longing and it seemed to

me that it was the eager breath of the summer seeking for its completion.

I knew not then that it was so near, that it was mine, and that this

Perfect sweetness had blossomed in the depth of my own heart.

—*Rabindranath Tagore, in* Earth Song

~

On the third day, she made herself get out of bed. She knew she had to eat something. She shuffled to the sink and filled a glass with water. Her head throbbed like the bass drum in a heavy metal band. She moved to the fridge and pulled the heavy door open. There were still two peach tarts wrapped snug on the top shelf. Oh, shoot! She forgot to send that recipe to Anna the skinny-voiced botanist. And the girl has the bridal shower this week. She glanced over her shoulder. Anna's card was still on the table where she'd left it three days ago. She took one of the tarts and the card over to the computer desk and settled in. The tart was gooey from too much time but still made her mouth happy. What she really needed was some coffee. She looked across the room at the forgotten carafe. It seemed so far away. But there was nothing for it. Maybe some caffeine would help this headache.

She got back up from the chair and went about the business of spooning the beans, grinding them to just the right consistency, measuring out the tap water. It wouldn't take long to brew. She glanced askance at the computer in the corner of the room. Why was she avoiding this?

She willed her feet to take her back to the tiny makeshift office. Sighed heavily. Sat down. Pulled up the email. Picking up the card, she carefully typed Anna's email address in the proper space.

Dear Anna,

She stared at the blank document for a minute.

I'm sorry for the delay in getting this recipe to you. I misplaced your card and only just came across it this morning…

It wasn't a total lie. She had just come across the card this morning. She needn't say it was because she'd been in bed for three days.

She tapped the delete button several times.

Dear Anna,

I'm sorry for the delay in getting this recipe to you. After the class left I found myself feeling a little down and am only just now finding the energy to follow-up on my promise.

At least that was honest. If not an understatement.

For this recipe, you will need:
extra virgin olive oil
2-3 medium shallots, thinly sliced
apple cider vinegar
kosher salt and black pepper
2 sheets frozen puff pastry, thawed

1 (8 ounce) wheel Brie each, cut into 8-10 slices (leave the rind on)
1/4 cup fresh basil, chopped
3 peaches, sliced
1 egg, beaten
1/3 cup honey
fresh chopped rosemary

She typed out the instructions for the tart from memory and hesitated at the end, but after considering, decided to include her phone number in case Anna had any questions. It was the polite thing to do. The recipe was easy and straightforward. She didn't expect there would be any questions. Not at all.

By the afternoon she was feeling almost human again, almost able to hold her head up, almost able to enter polite society. She even felt a little bit lonely. She was surprised to find her feet carrying her down the meadow path, making her way to the bees. She recalled, as she strode down the hill, a conversation she'd had with Corrie not long after they received the diagnosis.

"You will have to tell the bees," Corrie had said. "After I'm gone."

"What?" She'd almost giggled, thinking it a joke—Corrie's way of making the heavy light.

"Yep. It's a tradition. The bees must be told when there is a death in the family. Some people say the news must be sung. Some will drape black cloth over the hives. You don't need to do all that. But you will have to tell them. Otherwise, they'll wonder."

She had told Corrie to hush. Said she didn't want to think of such things. *Tell the bees, indeed.* Most days, she had to tell herself. Be reminded. It was too easy to drift along, pretend.

She shook her head to shake off the thoughts. Turned her mind to the bees.

If she decided to keep them, she would have to deal with harvesting the honey very soon. Rhoda was clear on that. She wasn't sure she was up to it if she was honest with herself. All the honey, all the sweet … all that would remind her heart of Corrie. And though she didn't want to forget, she knew she couldn't keep living in the land of dreams and poetry.

When she arrived at the clearing, there wasn't much to see. She didn't want to suit up, so she sat in the grass at a distance, watched a few foragers come and go. The goldenrod was nectaring, she could tell by the way the plush, yellow heads of the flowers bent under the weight. The bees were getting their fill, she could hear the steady hum of hundreds of wings settle over the meadow. She leaned back into the thick grass and closed her eyes, let herself fall into the hum and the sky and the scent of green.

~

When she got back to the house there were three missed calls on her phone. She knew who one would be, stared at the name in anger and frustration. They called every day now. Except Sundays. And just one time a day. No message, not even a cursory one. She couldn't explain the red-hot anger that appeared behind her eyes every time she saw the name. Didn't even want to try. She didn't even hesitate before deleting that call with one swipe of her finger. She didn't recognize the other number, assumed a telemarketer. But it was unusual for the junk callers to call twice. And they'd left messages, apparently. She lifted the phone to her ear.

"Ah, uh, yeah, this is Anna, from the beekeeping class? I wanted to thank you for the recipe and …"

Was she crying? There was definitely a catch in the young woman's voice.

"… and, I hate to ask, but do you … do you think you could come to my place and show me how to put these tarts together? I've been trying a test batch all morning and I can't even get this puff pastry to work for me, and I …" She let out a sort of gulp and sob at the same time. "I hate to ask, but the shower is tomorrow, and I wanted it to be so special and I just keep messing everything up. I'm so sorry. I'm such a mess. Will you please call me back? Thank you."

The second call was designed to make up for the desperation of the first one, she presumed.

"Hi, there, this is Anna again. I just wanted to apologize for my earlier call. I feel so silly. Please, please, disregard it, okay? And don't feel like you have to call me back. I'll just eliminate the tarts from my menu. It will be fine. Thank you so much for trying to help. I appreciate it more than you can know."

No tears in the second call but she could hear the disappointment in Anna's voice. The tarts were going to be the star of her menu. And now it would just be cucumber sandwiches and mints. The poor child.

She sighed and hit "call back" before she could change her mind.

~

"Rhoda told me you used to run a catering bizness?" Anna was talking with her mouth full again. *Had she never been told?* She was beginning to see that Anna never did only one thing at a time. Like chew. "That is so cool. Tell about it! I want to hear it all!"

She smiled and checked herself, surprised to realize she was having fun. She brushed egg white on the edges of the tarts and considered her words. Anna's eyes followed her every move, but all she had done in the kitchen so far was nibble away on the sliced brie.

"I did! I ran The Indigo Kitchen for twenty years. It was … a dream come true. Also, stressful."

"The Indigo Kitchen! Yes, I remember. The blue food truck, right? I used to see that thing all over town. What kind of food did you make? When did you stop doing it? And why?"

She laughed, "Woah, woah, woah! One question at a time. My introvert brain doesn't work that fast."

"What kind of food?"

"Whatever my client wanted."

Anna looked skeptical.

"So, what, just, anything?"

"Well, yeah. I had my specialties, of course. But I've been to culinary school, so I can do about anything."

"What were your specialties?"

She slid the tarts in the preheated oven and wiped her hands on her apron. "Hmmm. Well, things like these peach tarts. What I would call, 'fresh, high country' food. Think … hmmm … like Ina Garten. I specialized in using food that was in season and locally sourced."

"Fresh high country. Never heard that term before."

"That's because I just made it up."

They both laughed and Anna reached for a leftover peach. She tossed it up and down in one hand, focusing her eyes on the up and down motion.

"Do you mind if I ask? Why did you give it up?"

She shrugged, untied the apron, slipped it over her head.

"Corrie got sick. I didn't have time to be a nurse and a chef."

"That must have been hard."

"Not really. I'd do the same thing again. It wasn't much of a sacrifice, considering."

"What about now? Don't you miss it?"

She leaned her backside against the counter and cocked her head, considering. "Sometimes I do. But five years is a long time to be away from something. I'm not the same person I was. Taking care of someone you love who is dying has a way of changing you. I don't know if I have it in me anymore."

Anna took a bite out of the peach she had been playing with. "Well, if dese darts are any indication," she swallowed, sucked in a rill of peach juice trailing her chin, "Then I'd say you do."

"Maybe," she smiled at Anna. "Maybe. It did feel good to be in the kitchen again. To make something for other people's pleasure."

Anna leaned in. "Yes! And I can't thank you enough. I'm always a disaster in the kitchen. But, that day at your house … you made these tarts look so simple. I always think things will be easier than they are. Sooo…I don't know why I freaked out the way I did. I just wanted this to be so special. I only have one sister. I'm so happy for her. I just wanted it to be…"

"It's perfectly fine! I'm glad to help. I should be thanking you. There aren't many things I enjoy right now…"

Anna held her with her eyes. "I can't imagine how hard it must be to find your way forward. I remember how Corrie would sometimes tell stories about the two of you in class. It was so evident—so real—the love there…"

She felt her eyes smarting. A wave of gratitude lapped up around the shores of her heart. She reached out for Anna's hand, returned the younger woman's burning stare. "Thank you."

4

She lifted the garage door with a great, heaving grunt. The contents of the tiny building looked like a time capsule. Everything just as she'd left it five years ago. When they'd parked the truck and never looked back.

There were some things she could never forget. Scent of fried dough mingled with the aroma of a dark Ethiopian blend in the morning. The bright yellow-gold of the meadowlark. Corrie, behind the wheel, head thrown back, laughing.

Swallowing, she felt for the keys in her pocket. She walked over to Little Indigo and peered in the window. Neat as a pin, just as she'd left it. She pulled the keys out of her pocket and opened the door; slid behind the wheel, then slid the key into the ignition and turned. Nothing.

"Dead battery," she muttered to herself. "What did I expect?"

She turned the key back to the off position and sat still for a moment, gripping both sides of the steering wheel and letting out a slow exhale. She hadn't realized she'd been holding her breath.

Am I really going to do this?

She got out her cell phone and punched up a number. "Yes, hello? Bri? Yes, it's just me…I'm fine, thanks for asking. I never did thank you for the peaches you sent…Mm Hmmm. Delicious. I made some tarts with them and still had plenty left to snack on. Oh, yeah? You'll have to give me the recipe… Hey, listen, when the boys come tomorrow to mow the grass, will you ask Caleb to bring his jumper cables? I've got a dead battery here and I don't know the first thing…Oh, thank you! I appreciate it so much. Yes. Okay, then. I'll let you get back to your preserves. Thanks again. Bye, bye now."

She hung up and continued staring through the windshield at nothing.

I guess I am. I guess I am going to do this.

~

She heard the mowers before she realized the guys had arrived, then threw a glance at the clock on her bedside table: 7:45. Those boys sure did believe in making hay while the sun was shining. She groaned deeply, stretched her arms above her head and swung her legs over the edge of the bed, pushing the covers aside. It was still hard to make herself get up in the morning, but she knew Caleb would want to jump the truck and be on his way to his next client. The Brown boys—not so much boys anymore, what was Caleb now? Twenty-six, twenty-seven? And Junebug not far behind him. Early twenties?—had amassed quite the landscaping business in the past few years. They were hard workers. And smart. Especially Caleb. That boy could do anything with his hands. Repair any kind of equipment, build anything, grow anything, make any kind of house-repair anyone could ever need…He had expanded the lawn-mowing business he started in high school to a full-fledged landscaping architecture practice without even trying. Everything he touched turned into something beautiful. He had a way of seeing. Corrie had had that same gift. Vision. A way of looking into the future and seeing how things would grow together.

She shook her head. Walked to the closet and pulled on the same jeans and T-shirt she'd worn yesterday, abandoned on the floor last night. She padded into the kitchen and got the coffee going, checked her phone for any messages, and waved to Junebug through the kitchen window. June was always the weed eater handler. He lifted his hand to her without missing a beat. The two of them could finish the wide expanse of her yard in just over half an hour. The coffeemaker beeped. She glanced at the clock before getting out three mugs and setting them on a tray. Caleb took his black, but she splashed some cream in the bottom of hers and June's before backing out the screen door, carefully balancing the tray, just as the mower quieted. She set the tray down on the table and took her place on the porch swing, waiting for the boys to join her, like they used to before she'd found it too hard to meet them here.

Caleb appeared first, wiping sweat from his brow despite the chill in the morning air that whispered fall. He wordlessly stooped to pick up his mug and sat down in the rocking chair to her left. He took a deep drink, closed his eyes and let out a sigh.

"I've missed this. 'Bout time you got that lazy butt out of bed. One of these days you're going to tell me your secret to making a plain old cup of coffee taste like a little bit of heaven."

She smiled. "You know I can't give away trade secrets. If you didn't leave before the sun came up you might have time for caffeine before you go."

"Then I'd miss out on the best cup of coffee this side of the Mississippi."

She raised her brows. "Only this side?"

He laughed as his brother joined them, taking his place beside her on the swing. He scooped his mug with both hands.

"You," Junebug said, lifting his mug in salute, "are a lifesaver."

She chuckled and said, "You're welcome."

"Mom said you need a jump? What you been doing to that Subaru to kill so young a battery?"

She kept her eyes on her coffee mug, cradled in her lap.

"It's not the Subaru what needs the jump."

She lifted her eyes to meet his. His honey eyes were dancing.

"You're finally getting Little Indigo out."

She smiled shyly and looked away, nodding.

Junebug slapped his leg, sloshing coffee onto his knee. "Yee-haw! It's about time!" He leaned over and planted a happy kiss on her cheek.

"It doesn't mean anything, boys, I'm just getting her out of storage and cleaning her up," she protested.

But they both beamed at her silently.

"I mean it!" she said. "Don't go getting any big ideas."

"Just in time for fried green tomatoes," Caleb teased. She swatted at his arm.

"I'm just getting the truck started. For now. That's all."

The boys looked knowingly at each other and simultaneously said, "For now."

"Are you going to help me or not?" she snapped.

"I brought my cables. What are we waiting for?" Caleb took another deep swig of his coffee and stood up. But before they could walk over to the garage, someone pulled into her driveway.

"You expecting company at," June looked at his watch, "8:37 a.m.?"

She peered at the Prius pulling up her long driveway and recognized Anna behind the wheel.

"No, I…well, I wonder what she needs?"

"Friend of yours?" Caleb asked.

"Sort of, I guess. A botanist that came by with Rhoda's class to help with the bees. I helped her with a wedding shower for her sister and I…Oh, never mind. Let me see what's up."

Anna parked beside Caleb's truck and approached the porch, carrying a basket. She glanced nervously at the two young men, her eyes taking in the tray with the mugs. She looked scared to death.

"Hi, Anna, what a nice surprise!" She called from the porch swing. "Is everything all right?"

Anna started a little at her voice. "Oh! Yes, I…I hope I'm not interrupting. I was determined to master those tarts you made for me and was up early baking. I thought I'd bring some by and get your opinion." She held out the basket.

"Tarts?" June perked up. "Well, if it's taste-testers you're needing, Miss, my brother and I are experts." He swooped down off the porch and scooped the basket from her hands, parting the tea towel that covered the top. "Let's see what we have here."

She could have sworn Anna was blushing. "I didn't know you'd have company, I'm so sorry…I just, well, you know how…"

"No worries, Anna! Won't you join us? Would you like a cup of coffee? Meet Caleb and Junebug." She gestured to the young men accordingly. "They're just the hired help." She stifled a smile. Junebug playfully punched her side the same time as he lifted a peach tart out of the basket now resting on the coffee tray. "June wasn't kidding. These boys have been my taste-testers since they were knee-high to a grasshopper."

Anna wavered on the walkway. "I-I don't want to interrupt."

"You're not interrupting! Oh, but wait. I forget myself. Caleb, do you guys have time to have a tart and some more coffee before helping me with the truck and getting on with your workday?"

Caleb was looking at Anna, his face unreadable.

"How could I possibly say no to a peach tart?" He drawled, not taking his eyes off Anna.

Anna was definitely blushing.

5

Her three coffee mates ended up staying until well after noon. Caleb and Junebug pronounced Anna's tarts as "brilliant." They *were* pretty good. The guys talked Anna into staying to help with the truck, Caleb rarely taking his eyes from the younger woman's, Anna blushing under his stare. Even after twenty minutes of jumping, the truck refused to start. Caleb offered to drive down to AutoWorks and buy a new battery, casually asking Anna if she wanted to accompany him. June headed over to the next lawn client, content to do the job on his own. "It's a small job," he said, grinning at his brother and Anna, winking in her direction.

Smiling shyly, Anna went with Caleb.

Will wonders never cease.

~

"Tell me everything you know about Caleb," Anna said, for the hundredth time. They were cleaning the inside of Little Indigo, sweeping up five years of dead insects, dust, and spiderwebs. And whatever this layer of crud was she couldn't seem to get off the windows. She rolled her eyes.

"I told you. Ask him whatever you want to know yourself. I'm not in the habit of talking about my friends behind their backs."

"Oh, come on! You know what I mean. I had so. Much. Fun. With him yesterday. And those eyes of his…" Anna clasped her hands together and did a little twirl. Right in front of the grill.

She rolled her eyes again. "Let it not be said that I hindered true love."

"Spill it."

"There's not much to tell, really. Caleb and Junebug… their parents own the farm just down the road."

"The big red barn?"

"Yeah. Their dad was a coal miner…"

"Was?"

"Yeah. Danny passed away—oh, seven or eight years ago? Let's see. Caleb was 15. It's been eleven years. Wow. Time. He had lung cancer. Very aggressive. They've always had orchards. Apples. Pears. Peaches. And a big garden for produce. Their mom, Aubry—Bri, we call her—has a produce stand during the summer and fall. She's the one who gave me the peaches for the tarts I made when we checked the hives. Anyway…"

"Is she nice? Their mom, I mean?"

"Oh, yes. When Corrie was sick, she made us a pie every single week. Her crust is better than mine. She's always been …good to us. Anyway. Caleb started mowing lawns for extra money to help his mom out after his dad died. He got some kind of landscape architecture certificate at the vocational school. He can grow anything. He and June incorporated their business about five years ago. It's really grown. They have a couple other guys who work for them. They are good boys."

She caught Anna's eye and held it.

"You could do a lot worse than Caleb."

"What about special friends? Is he seeing anyone?"

She frowned and rubbed the stubborn residue on the window harder. "Not that I know of. But I wouldn't. We don't talk about stuff like that. I don't think Caleb has time for dating. He's always onto the next big idea."

"What kind of big ideas?"

"Growing his business and growing things. A few years ago he helped work on getting a grant to put in some community gardens at the Episcopal church downtown. They have a homeless shelter and a food pantry he's on the board for. He works with the Master Gardeners on all kinds of volunteer work. Not too long ago he took some classes and added solar panel installation to his business. That's been doing surprisingly well. He's just always curious, always learning, always growing—no pun intended."

"He sounds lovely."

She turned to study Anna, the younger woman rubbing her homemade white vinegar cleaning solution over the surface Little Indigo's built-in stainless-steel grill. "What about you?"

Anna stopped, mid swipe. "What about me?"

"What's the story on your love life?"

Anna laughed, a high tinkling sound that somehow rang with sadness. "What love life? I haven't been on a date in two years."

She went back to her aggressive rubbing of the windows. "Why not?"

Anna sighed. "I suppose I could make up an interesting story about my jilted lover, but the truth is, no one has asked. My life…it doesn't leave a lot of room for socializing. I teach, I do my research, I put in my time at the Naturalist program…"

"You help rescue neglected bee hives. You," she stopped wiping the windows for a minute, back still to Anna, "help grieving matrons remember who they are."

There was a pause, a stillness behind her.

"Well…I don't know about…I can't take credit for that." She heard a smile in Anna's voice, resumed shining the windows.

"Why don't you ask him out?"

"Who? Me? Caleb?"

"Yeah. He's obviously very interested. He couldn't seem to take his eyes off you."

"Then why didn't he ask me out?"

"Why didn't you ask him?"

She could almost hear Anna's eye roll behind her back. "I don't know. I don't do stuff like that. Believe it or not, when it comes to guys, I'm kind of shy. And now, I don't have his number. And he didn't ask for mine."

"Maybe he's shy too."

"He didn't seem shy. He was just…fun. He's fun to be around."

She turned and smiled at her new friend. "If you want to get a hold of him, you can always leave a message at his landscaping business. Google it. It's called Greensky."

Anna looked thoughtful. "Greensky? Hmm." Anna stilled her wiping. "Maybe I need some kind of lawn consultation."

~

It was the poem by Claude McKay that did it. "I shall return again," the poem began. And that was all it took.

I shall return again; I shall return
To laugh and love and watch with wonder-eyes
At golden noon the forest fires burn,
Wafting their blue-black smoke to sapphire skies.
I shall return to loiter by the streams
That bathe the brown blades of the bending grasses,
And realize ...

Realize what? If Corrie returned to her now, what would they do? They'd had so many plans they hadn't been able to realize. That trip to Europe. Retiring near the ocean. They'd hoped for grandkids one day.

And realize once more my thousand dreams...

So many more than a thousand dreams with Corrie.

She fell asleep in her reading chair, counting all the dreams she lost when she lost Corrie.

Of waters rushing down the mountain passes.
I shall return to hear the fiddle and fife
Of village dances, dear delicious tunes
That stir the hidden depths of native life,
Stray melodies of dim remembered runes.
I shall return, I shall return again,
To ease my mind of long, long years of pain.

The next morning, she was wakened by the phone. Her back was going to pay for sleeping in the chair. She stood up and stretched, making no effort to grab the phone, ringing ceaselessly from where she'd dropped it on the kitchen table yesterday.

Yep. Her back was not happy. She heard the notification indicating someone had left a voicemail, then moved to the counter to start making the coffee. The bright side of falling asleep in the chair? She was already dressed for the day. Maybe she would even brush her teeth. But first: coffee.

She shuffled over to the table and picked up her phone. Two voicemail messages. Couldn't a person even sleep in on a Tuesday morning? Rhoda and Anna. She had never been so popular.

She punched up the first message.

"Hey, girl. It's me, Rhoda. Wondering how the bees are doing. We're expecting our first frost this week so thought I'd remind you to prepare some extra food for them. Just peek in and see how the honey stores are holding up. Since the nectar supplies are getting scarce you may need to give a little help. Do you know how to make the sugar syrup? I use the plastic bag method. I think Corrie did too. Anyway. Give me a call if you need some help."

Anna's trill voice came through when she tapped the second message.

"Hey, you. Guess who has a lawn consultation scheduled with our favorite landscape architect? I'm so excited but also scared to death. I mean, my yard is the size of a postage stamp. He's going to know I just wanted to see him. Tell me I'm not crazy, okay? Ugh! I'm going insane. Call me back and give me a pep talk, okay? He's coming this evening!"

She couldn't help smiling at Anna's manic excitement. But she didn't feel like talking to anyone. Not after last night's poetry pity party. Maybe she would check on the bees first. She didn't really know how to do the sugar water or what in the world the plastic bag method was, but that's what Google was for, right? Plus, Corrie had a bazillion bee books at her disposal. She dipped in the fridge for the half and half, splashed a little in yesterday's dirty mug and poured herself a cup of coffee, then sat down in front of the computer and typed in the search engine, "Sugar water for honeybees."

An hour later she was more confused than when she started. Apparently, not all beekeepers believed giving bees sugar water is a good thing. But most agree it is better than letting your bees starve. From what she could tell, experienced beekeepers could determine if their bees needed supplemental sugar water by the weight of the hive. Most of the articles she read said bees need 50-60 pounds of honey to make it through the winter. She would have to remove the supers—the honey collected for harvesting—before offering the sugar water, or it would affect her yield. The syrup itself was easy enough to make and feed the bees, but she couldn't shake the fear she would do something wrong.

She scratched her head and tried to ward off the irritability. *Beekeeping is obviously best learned through doing it.* She hated the thought of calling Rhoda again. She sighed and got up from the chair, refreshed her coffee and moved to the window.

~

It wasn't as hard as the internet made it seem. She climbed out of the bee suit and hung it on the hook in the shed. Thank goodness for YouTube. She peered out the window at Corrie's hives and felt an unfamiliar feeling stir in her breast. What was this? Could it be… pride? She chuckled to herself. Wouldn't Corrie get a kick out of this? She was *proud* of herself. She'd figured out the sugar water thing all by herself. Well, with YouTube, anyway. And she'd been able to get a good look at all the hives while she was feeding them. Everyone seemed perfectly fine. She sat down at Corrie's desk and opened the record book. On the first blank page she wrote the date. Next to that she wrote, "Gallon bags of sugar-water for all seven hives." She smoothed her fingers over Corrie's small, neat penmanship. Inside this little book was all the information she needed to take care of these bees. No matter how much energy the treatments stole, Corrie always managed to visit the bees. Until those final few months, anyway. She flipped back to this day, one year ago.

"Unseasonably cold this week. Tonight's forecast calling for our first freeze. All the hives felt light so I made some sugar-water feeders. Everyone should be fat and happy."

She laughed out loud. Fat and happy, indeed. Oh, Corrie.

She closed the book softly and tucked it to her breast, carrying it close to her heart as she made her way back up to the house.

That night she read through years of Corrie's beekeeping notes, hoping that through some kind of magic osmosis Corrie's talent with the bees would drift up through the pages, into her fingers and through her body. *Do bees recognize their keepers? Were Corrie's bees aware a stranger was in their midst?*

She closed the notebook and rubbed her eyes. She was tired. But it was still too early for bed. She picked up *Earth Song* and thumbed her way to the latest dog-eared page.

The New Moon

Day, you have bruised and beaten me,
As rain beats down the bright, proud sea,
Beaten my body, bruised my soul,
Left me nothing lovely or whole—
Yet I have wrested a gift from you,
Day that dies in dusky blue:

For suddenly over the factories
I saw a moon in the cloudy seas—
A wisp of beauty all alone
In a world as hard and gray as stone—
Oh who could be bitter and want to die
When a maiden moon wakes up in the sky?

—Sara Teasdale

Such a sweet poem. On a whim, she lifted her tired body from the chair and went out on the porch. Where was the moon tonight? She walked down the steps and craned her neck, tilting her head up to the sky. It was already cold, and she hugged herself tightly as her eyes adjusted to the dark. It was a clear night and the stars winked brightly above her. She could readily pick out the Big Dipper and Cassiopeia, but here in the quiet of her country home the stars bled together like glitter-dust. It so happened that they were close to the new moon. Funny that. She scanned the eastern horizon. There it was— "wisp of beauty all alone." Small, scant, like a thin-lipped smile. She thought about how the moon does this every month, starts over. Growing and diminishing and growing again. It made her tired to think about.

She liked this tiny moon; thought it beautiful, even. She wasn't a fool. She knew there was more. She knew the largest part of the moon lay hidden in shadow. But this tiny sliver was lovely. Was she wrong to dread the coming changes? Did the moon fear the reveal of gradual illumination each month?

She breathed warmly into cupped hands and watched the breath lift away from her in vapor. As she made her way back into the house, she remembered this: there is always one side of the moon turned away from the earth, cloaked in shadow.

Maybe someone should write a poem about that.

6

Anna and Caleb were dating now, it seemed.

"I was showing him around my little greenhouse, trying to, you know, pretend I needed some ideas about how to make it less researchy and more, um, attractive, and the next thing I know, he's kissing me underneath my giant Anthurium clarinervium."

Anna's face was pink, slightly glowing. "Am I crazy? I mean, I don't move that fast. I like to be...sure...of people before I let myself start to hope about a relationship and I, well, Caleb's been over every night this week and I haven't gotten any work done for days and I don't even seem to care." Anna plopped down on the plushy bench seat tucked behind the cab of Little Indigo. "What is wrong with me?"

She suppressed a smile but continued stocking the pantry as Anna prattled. A shipment of stock items from one of her favorite suppliers in New York had just arrived. Something was singing inside her as she handled these once familiar foodstuffs. She put all the different types of flours in her see-through, airtight plastic canisters. She preferred glass but when you cook in a kitchen on wheels you learn the value of lightweight and shatter proof. She tucked the canisters in the rack above the stand mixer: AP flour, pastry flour, cake flour, 00 flour (maybe this would be the year she installed that ceramic pizza oven), bread flour...She turned back to the shipping box and dipped her hands in. And these spices! You couldn't get spices like these around here. She neatly lined up the small glass bottles, arranging them alphabetically in her spice rack: amchoor powder, black cardamon, blade mace, charnuska…

"Are you even listening to me?"

She studied the orderly display with quiet satisfaction. "It sounds to me like you might be falling in love." *Maybe that would shut her up.*

When Anna didn't respond, she finally turned around to face her. The girl's pink flush had turned to a pale, greenish cast just under her skin.

"Love?" she said, weakly. "Love isn't something that can happen this fast."

She glanced reluctantly over her shoulder at the neat rows of spices, the half-full box, before stepping over to the bench and sitting next to Anna.

"I fell in love with Corrie the first time we met."

Anna raised a skeptical eyebrow. "Really? And when was that?"

"Second grade. Miss Kovalan's class. Corrie had just moved here from New Jersey. Our eyes met that first day and that was it for me."

"Oh, come on. Didn't you two grow up and marry other people?"

She shifted her gaze back over to the spice rack. All those bottles. So perfectly ordered.

She drew a deep breath and nodded. "Yes, we did. That's…"

Her next words were interrupted by a loud banging on the window.

"Anybody home?" A voice called loudly from outside. Anna's face flushed pink again.

Suppressing another smile, she got up and opened the window, lifted the sash and propped up the canopy. Caleb's grinning face filled the frame. "May I take your order, sir?"

He leaned in and, catching Anna's eye, said, "I'll have one Anna Lynnette Ferris. To go, please."

"Caleb!" Anna's cheeks had bright red splotches on them now.

Caleb laughed, shameless. "Seriously… I have a surprise free afternoon—city planning meeting was canceled at the last minute. I was driving by and saw Anna's car. Can you spare her?" He turned back to Anna. "I have some more ideas for that greenhouse of yours."

~

Back in the house, she was alone again. She mustered a mild irritation when she saw the expected 11:00 a.m. missed call. She deleted it unceremoniously and flopped down in her reading chair, then picked up *Earth Song* and balanced it delicately on her lap. To sit and savor the poems always felt like transcending time and space. She opened the book to a dog-eared page.

Wood Song

I heard a wood thrush in the dusk
*   Twirl three notes and make a star—*
My heart that walked with bitterness
*   Came back from very far.*

Three shining notes were all he had,
And yet they made a starry call—
I caught life back against my breast
And kissed it, scars and all.

—*Sara Teasdale*

She stared at the words blankly for a moment. *Scars and all.* She closed the book softly and walked over to the window. Four does were grazing on the back lawn. Two of them looked like yearlings. She studied the graceful lines of their bodies, watched their ears and their tails twitch, communicating silently with one another. She leaned her forehead into the cool pane of the window.

"But I don't want these scars," she breathed softly, letting her breath fog the glass. She felt so lonely, so alone. Before the emptiness could take hold of her, her phone rang. She startled and returned to the chair where she'd left the darn thing. She glanced at the name before answering.

"Hi, there."

"Hey, Number Two."

She smiled at the familiar nickname. She knew most step-moms rarely earn a fond one, let alone second to first. She would never take her place in Sarah's life for granted.

"Hi, Sarah. What's up?"

"I was feeling lonely today and thought you might be too. How are things?"

How to answer?

"Oh, things are going along. You know."

"I guess I do. Hey, a little bird told me you've gotten Little Indigo out."

"How in the world did you hear about that?"

"I ran into Caleb at a school board meeting. He's already talking about your fried catfish sandwiches."

"Oh, Lordy. What was Caleb doing at a school board meeting? You'd think that boy has better things to do than gossip about me. I'm just cleaning her up. Stocking some pantry items. I don't have any big plans."

"You know Caleb. He was introducing a gardening-in-the-classroom project. The board loved it. And as far as big plans, well, that's what I was calling about. The school is putting on a fall festival next month to raise money for our new play-ground. We're inviting some local food trucks to be a part. I thought it might be a good way to break Little Indigo back in. Plus, good cause and all."

She was silent for a moment, a lump forming in her throat.

"Sarah…I don't know. I don't know if I…if I could do that by myself."

"But that's the good part. The festival is on a Saturday. So I won't be teaching. I thought I could be your driver. And your sous chef. If you'll have me. I know I have…big shoes to fill."

Tears were streaming down her face. "Oh, sweetheart. How can I say no to that?"

7

"So we have, what? Three and a half weeks to get ready?"

She was growing accustomed to Anna dropping by unannounced. The younger woman didn't seem to mind being put to work. If she was permitted to prattle on, that is.

"Yes, Sarah's coming over tonight to look through recipes with me so we can come up with a menu. What do you mean, 'we'?"

Anna dipped her rag in the bucket of soapy water and continued wiping down the porch railings.

"Haven't I been in on this with you from the beginning? Don't you think I should be present on Little Indigo's maiden voyage?"

She noticed the white paint was peeling off the railings where she had vigorously scoured a moldy spot with the scrub brush. She frowned.

"Do you think Caleb would give this porch a new coat of paint for me? I never noticed how tired looking it's become."

"I doubt that Mr. Busybody would have time for that. What with all the meetings he's been going to lately. He might get one of the guys who works for him do it, though."

They worked on in silence for a few minutes before Anna picked it back up.

"So, how about it? You and me and Sarah in Little Indigo for the fall festival?"

She straightened up and turned to face Anna.

"Anna, no offense, sweetheart, but I've noticed you aren't

much help in the kitchen."

Anna smirked.

"You speak wisdom, oh sage one, but who will take the orders? Who will handle the cash? Don't you need someone out front while you and Sarah slave away over the grill?"

She rubbed the back of her neck with her right hand, considering. "Hmm. You might be right. Corrie always took the orders and helped me in the kitchen when necessary. But with Sarah's inexperience, that might be a little tricky for her. It's just that there's not a lot of room to move around in there. Three people could get a little bumpy."

"I can be very small. You won't even know I'm there."

"Let me think about it. Maybe we could try it out some time before-hand and see how it goes."

"Like tonight! I've been wanting to meet Sarah anyway. After we plan the menu we can head out to Little Indigo and see how it feels with three of us."

She was silent for a moment. She had kind of been looking forward to having Sarah to herself for a little bit. But she was also nervous. They hadn't been together since the days immediately following the funeral. She really didn't want to talk about Corrie tonight. Maybe it wasn't a bad idea to have someone else there to buffer all those emotions. She dropped the scrub brush into the bucket.

"You know, for someone who's too shy to ask a guy out, you sure are good at inviting yourself into other folks' stuff. Don't you and Caleb have anything to do together tonight?" She knew they'd been spending every evening together.

Anna was close to a pout. "He has a city planning meeting tonight. Says they always run late."

She studied the girl's forlorn face. "Oh, all right."

Anna gave a little jump of glee. "Yay!"

"Come at 5:30. And bring a bag of tortilla chips. I'm making enchiladas."

~

"I sure have missed your cooking," Sarah said, after swallowing a bite of enchilada. She, at least, knew not to talk with her mouth full.

But Anna, too, was on her best behavior—taking small nibbles off her plate, daintily dipping a tortilla chip into the bowl of home-canned salsa, remaining uncharacteristically quiet. If she didn't know better, she would think Anna was nervous.

"Aww, thanks, honey. This is one of the recipes I thought we might consider for the festival. A Mexican theme is relatively easy and fairly inexpensive to put together. We'd have more profits for the playground fund."

"That sounds like a good idea to me! What else would be on the menu?"

"We could have some street tacos…beans and rice, of course, maybe some nachos, churros for the sweet tooth… avocado and chicken tortas would be easy, even huaraches would be cool."

"Where-what-cheez?" Anna giggled, with her mouth full (of course).

"Huaraches. It's like a Mexican pizza."

"Never heard of it," Anna said. "Maybe that's good. People might be curious."

"I like that idea," Sarah said. "But we probably don't need that many menu items. What do you think would sell best?"

"At a grade school fall festival? We should probably just make cheese quesadillas and be done with it."

"Oh, come now!" Sarah teased. "A lot of our parents have more sophisticated palettes than that! Some of the children do too."

"I loved Mexican food when I was little!" Anna exclaimed. "Oh, the warm churros." She put her hand on her stomach and leaned back in her chair dreamily.

Sarah shifted her gaze to Anna and studied her closely. "Did you grow up around here, Anna? You must be close to me and Caleb in age, but I don't remember you from school."

Anna abruptly straightened back up in her chair and shifted uncomfortably. "I did. But you wouldn't have seen me in school." She took a deep breath. "I grew up in St. Virgil's. We had our own school there."

She stopped mid-chew and fixed her eyes on Anna too, trying not to show her surprise. "Anna! You never told me that."

"St. Virgil's," Sarah mused. "Do you mean the—"

"Group home on the south side?" Anna interrupted. "Yep. Home sweet home for me and Aida since I was nine and she was five. Aida was adopted when she was six, but her family made sure we stayed close."

"But how did you end up there, Anna? And why didn't Aida's family take you too?"

"Our parents died in a motorcycle accident, and we didn't have any other family. I had some... er... special needs that prevented me from being placed in the foster care system, which is usually how kids went on to be adopted." She looked up at both sets of eyes staring at her.

"What kind of special needs?" They asked, simultaneously.

Anna lowered her eyes and tucked her chin into her chest slightly. "I was born with a heart condition. I had to have surgery to correct the problem when I was an infant. I needed a special valve to make my heart work right and two years later the valve failed. I had to have another surgery to have it replaced. Usually, they last a lot longer than that, but we knew I would need more surgery as I grew. My medical history was enough to spook potential fosters. St. Virgil's decided to just keep me there so they could provide for my medical expenses."

As she studied Anna's face, a coldness crept into her heart. "But you're okay now, right, Anna?"

Anna lifted her eyes and met her gaze. She smiled. "Yes. I'm good now. I have regular check-ups with my cardiologist, of course. And if I so much as feel a little bit winded they want me to come in ASAP. But I'm in good shape and take good care of myself."

She felt a rush of relief and to her embarrassment, tears. "I'm so glad to hear that."

Anna's mouth formed a tiny "O" at the tears. She shifted in her seat and reached over to clasp her hand.

"Hey, now. It's okay. It's just like I said, I'm fine now. I didn't mean to spring all that on you like that. Sorry about that. I don't usually like to talk about it because people start acting all weird and stuff when they find out I'm an orphan and have this weird heart thing. But St. Virgil's was a cool place to grow up. They gave me the care I needed. The sisters were good to me. It's because of them I fell in love with botany. They still have the most beautiful gardens in town. I started learning about hybridizing roses when I was twelve years old. It kind of saved my life."

She squeezed Anna's hand. "That's what cooking did for me. Is still doing. And I'm sorry to be so emotional. I just kind of like you, that's all."

Anna's face was glowing. "Well, I kind of like you too."

Sarah chuckled. "I'm beginning to feel like a third wheel!"

They all laughed, and Anna leaned back in her chair with a sigh. She closed her eyes and placed her hand on her stomach. "That was soo good. Now, if only we had some of those peach tarts …"

"Aren't you tired of those yet? I didn't make a dessert because I thought we might try out the churros recipe in the truck by way of testing out the space. But … let me see what I have in here."

She jumped up and peered in the cupboard. She pulled out a box of Ritz crackers and tossed them on the table. Then she opened the fridge and came back with some Laughing Cow cheeses and a jar of apricot jam.

Sarah grinned. "The Bethany!"

Anna wrinkled her brow. "The Bethany?"

She grinned. "Yeah. It's a delicacy named after a friend from culinary school." She carefully removed the foil from three tiny triangles of cheese. "Once a week we would have dinner at Bethany's place—kind of a way of letting off steam after the intensity of the classes. After a week of making fancy dishes, we'd all bring one thing from our pantry and see what we could throw together. It was kind of like, Survivor meets Chopped." She pulled out a cracker, spread a spoonful of apricot jam over it and topped it with a piece of cheese. "This was one of our all-time favorite creations."

She handed the cracker to Anna, who popped the whole thing in her mouth at once. "Mmm. Not bad," she said, with her mouth full. "Not quite the level of the peach tart, but it will do in a pinch. And I think I can definitely make this recipe!"

They finished an entire sleeve of Ritz crackers before heading out to Little Indigo to make some churros.

8

The weeks went fast and the days faster. Anna and Sarah came over every Friday night and Saturday morning and the three of them practiced their cooking routine. The menu was set: enchiladas, avocado tortas, nachos, sides of beans and rice, and, of course, churros. They decided to do a dry run the Saturday before the festival to iron out any wrinkles. She had gotten a permit to park the truck just off Main Plaza downtown.

Little Indigo was stocked and ready to go, but when the morning of the dry run arrived, she couldn't get out of bed.

She heard Sarah let herself in with her key and call softly for her through the kitchen.

"In here," she responded weakly from the bed.

Sarah appeared in the doorway. She crossed her arms and leaned against the frame. "What are you doing, Number Two? Why aren't you up and dressed already?"

"I …" Her reply was interrupted by the slam of the screen door. Anna's voice echoed down the hall.

"Hello?"

Anna's face appeared behind Sarah. "Wait. What's going on?"

The dim light of morning whispered through the curtains, making light play across the ceiling. "I'm not going. I don't feel up to it. You two go without me."

There was a brief silence before she heard movement in the doorway. "No, no, no, no," Anna said. "Sarah, you make some coffee. I'll deal with this." She heard Sarah pad down the hallway. Anna came over and sat down on the bed beside her. With great effort she moved her eyes from the ceiling to the face of her young friend. "I mean it, Anna. I don't think I can do this."

Anna reached for her hand and clasped it in both of hers. "And that is exactly why you must."

She closed her eyes and let the tears roll down her cheeks. Anna leaned over and wiped them away with the corner of the bedsheet. "Hey? You know what I did when I was nine years old and missed my mom? I planted something in the garden. The sisters gave me my own supply of seeds. It got a little easier each time. Remember how you said cooking was saving you?"

She nodded, slowly.

"Okay then. Let it. Let it keep doing the hard work of saving."

She drew in a shaky breath. "Okay."

Anna helped her get dressed the way a mother would help a child. Head through the neck hole. Thread the arms through. One leg at a time. Right sock. Left sock.

When it was done, she found she could move by her own volition. It was hard. She felt like she was crawling through water but she was moving. By the time they were loaded into Little Indigo and headed downtown, her limbs were a little lighter. And at the end of the lunch rush she had almost completely forgotten her earlier paralysis.

After the festival, she sat in the middle of the bench seat, Sarah driving, Anna gazing out the window. She was tired. But she felt a smile begin inside of her and gradually spread to her face. Anna, catching a change in her expression, bumped her with her shoulder. "Proud of you," she said, shifting her eyes back to the window.

"Thank you," she replied. "For everything."

~

The food truck festival was a huge success. Indigo Kitchen alone raised enough money for phase one of the playground construction. Altogether, enough funds were secured to get the project well underway. What's more, it served to jumpstart the reputation of The Indigo. She had brought along a stack of her old business cards and, at the end of the day, they were all gone.

She began receiving calls about private catering events.

It started with an open house for a realtor downtown. One of the teachers wanted something special for his wife's fiftieth birthday party. A group of actors at The City Theater celebrating the end of a show.

September faded into October. October gave way to November. And before she knew it, things were happening too fast to feel overwhelmed. She limited herself to one—no more than two—events a month. It was her nature to enjoy the planning as much as the event itself and she wanted to give herself time … time for pauses in between on her difficult days.

Sometimes the event was onsite and Little Indigo stayed parked in the garage. Sometimes Anna joined her, sometimes Sarah, sometimes both. But, for the most part, she was learning to handle things alone. And finding a quiet joy.

The Edge

I.

I thought to die that night in the solitude
  where they would never find me…
But there was time…
And I lay quietly on the drawn knees of the
  mountain staring into the abyss.

I do not know how long…
I could not count the hours, they ran so fast—
Like little bare-foot urchins—shaking my hands away.
But I remember
Somewhere water trickled like a thin severed vein
And a wind came out of the grass,
Touching me gently, tentatively, like a paw.

As the night grew
The gray cloud that had covered the sky like sackcloth
Fell in ashen folds about the hills,
Like hooded virgins pulling their cloaks about them…
There must have been a spent moon,
For the tall one's veil held a shimmer of silver. …

This too I remember,
And the tenderly rocking mountain,

Silence,
And beating stars. ….

II.

Dawn
Lay like a waxen hand upon the world,
And folded hills
Broke into a solemn wonder of peaks stemming clear
     and cold,
Till the Tall One bloomed like a lily,
Flecked with sun
Fine as a golden pollen.
It seemed a wind might blow it from the snow.

I smelled the raw sweet essences of things,
And heard spiders in the leaves,
And ticking of little feet
As tiny creatures came out of their doors
To see God pouring light into his star.
It seemed life held
No future and no past for me but this.

And I too got up stiffly from the earth
And held my heart up like a cup.

—*Lola Ridge*

She had taken to falling asleep in the honey field at least three times a week. Every time she read a poem like "The Edge" she tucked the words in her heart and headed down the hill. She was doing better about being—staying more connected to Anna and Sarah and Caleb and June, planning for all the events with Little Indigo, actually wearing clean clothes each day now. But sometimes, The Tired just took over. That was when only the company of the bees would do. She gave in to it, tying a new striped hammock between the two pin oaks standing sentinel over the meadow. The crisp fall afternoons were the perfect cradle, cloudless sky and slow-shedding leaves good companions. There, she hugged *Earth Song* to her breast and let poetry lull her into a dream-filled slumber. Corrie's hair, lifted by this same breeze caressing her face. Corrie's hands, covering hers. Corrie, head tilted to listen to the humming of the bees.

Today, she was having trouble leaving her little nest. How long had she been here?

> *I smelled the raw sweet essences of things,*
> *And heard spiders in the leaves,*
> *And ticking of little feet*
> *As tiny creatures came out of their doors*

The sun was beginning to lower behind the surrounding hills. Maybe she could stay out here all night. Wouldn't that be fun? Then she could watch God pouring light into his star.

But, no. They boys were coming to mow the meadow tomorrow. What would they think to discover her here? She smiled at the thought. They would think she had completely lost it. She sighed heavily and swung her legs out of the hammock.

And I too got up stiffly from the earth
And held my heart up like a cup.

~

She was awakened the next morning by a pounding on her door. Groaning softly, she turned over and looked at the clock. Seven-thirty. What the—?

The pounding persisted. She rolled out of bed and reached for her housecoat. "I'm coming, I'm coming," she called, as she made her way to the door.

She peered through the curtain and threw open the door. Caleb was standing on the porch, looking sheepish.

"Sorry to wake you but we've got a little problem down in the meadow."

"Problem?" She rubbed her eyes. "What sort of problem?"

"It's the bees. One of the hives has swarmed."

"What? That's not possible. This isn't the time of year for swarming. I've been keeping a close eye on them all. There's been nothing amiss as far as I—"

"Come and see for yourself. They're up in one of the pin oaks, right above your hammock. I'm not too concerned, but Junebug suggested we wait to commence mowing just in case it spooked them and they swarmed off. Where they are now, they'll be easy to collect. But you're gonna want to check out the hive and see what the issue is."

"Oh, for crying out loud. Let me get dressed. I'll call Rhoda and be right down."

Caleb hesitated on the porch.

"What?" she asked.

"You know you don't need to bother Rhoda, right? I've run across this before. I can capture them back for you if you like."

"Are you sure? Don't you have other work to do? What do you know about bees, Caleb?" She tried not to sound annoyed. She didn't want to lose any of Corrie's bees.

Caleb grinned, picking up on her stress. "Calm down. I know a pretty good bit about bees, thank you. I've been teaching a class on beekeeping at the tech center for two years. Rhoda isn't the only expert around, you know. I'm planning on starting my own apiary when I have the time. Right now, I've got my hands full with the ones the kids are tending at the center."

She felt so tired, felt her body let down the tension. "Oh, Caleb. Is there nothing you can't do? If you have time to help me, I will make it up to you. Somehow."

"Don't worry about it. But we do need to figure out what's going on. Do you have another hivebox in the shed? This swarm must want some more room. No sense putting them back in the old hive. They've probably started raising a new queen for those left behind anyway."

"I think so. Go on down and keep an eye on them. I'll get dressed and be right down."

"Bring a cardboard box if you have one. I have a nuc box in the truck if you don't."

9

Caleb had his own hood and gloves. He didn't bother donning the rest of the suit. They'd heard the steady humming of the swarm even before they were halfway down the hill. Now, she and Caleb stood beneath the thrum, necks arched in contemplation of the task. Caleb leaned the extension ladder up against the thick trunk of the oak and gestured for her to hold it steady. He held the box aloft with one hand as he ascended. She leaned her weight into the ladder and watched in wonder as a cloud of honeybees swirled around his head and lighted on a large cluster wrapped around the tip of a low branch. The swarm was about the size of a football and would easily fit in the box she'd found in her office area. She'd had to empty it of some old files Corrie had refused to part with— "just in case." She grinned a little at the label on the long side of the box: *B.*

Appropriate.

She shifted her attention back to Caleb as he hesitated for a moment. Somewhere inside the thrumming, pulsing cluster of honeymakers was the queen—safely sheltered by her fawning subjects. Caleb studied the swarm, trying to decide the gentlest way to move the bees. She knew he'd hoped to cut the branch and lower them into the box still attached. But she could see the limb was too thick for the handsaw he had tucked into his tool belt. He looked down at her, gave a quick shrug and, turning back toward the bees, deftly scooped the swarm into the box. Most of the bees stayed in formation and she heard an audible *bump!* before Caleb put the lid on. A few stragglers remained, but they followed the scent of their queen as Caleb descended, cradling the box against his side. He carried it over to the other hives and set it down in the grass.

She marveled at his calm confidence. Would she ever feel that comfortable around these critters?

"Let's leave them in the box overnight and give the strays a chance to find their hive," Caleb said, watching as a few worker bees climbed through the holes on the side of the cardboard box. "I'll come over tomorrow night at dusk and help you get them transferred to the new hivebox."

"Oh, Caleb. You are such a peach. How can I ever thank you enough?"

He smiled his acceptance of her gratitude. "No worries. I'll see if Anna wants to come help. She's almost done with Rhoda's class. She might find this interesting. We'll be over between six and six-thirty tomorrow."

"I'll make some chili. The least I can do is feed you."

"I've had your chili, so no arguments from me." He smiled. "Before I go, let's take a look into that abandoned hive and see if we can find evidence of the making of a new queen."

~

The next evening, Caleb wore his hood and gloves again. She had already assembled the new hivebox. It was ready and waiting for new tenants. Anna had clad herself in gear from head to toe, even though she stood back in the shadow of the shed—well away from the hives. Caleb did most of the work, carefully brushing the strays from the file box into the hive. When he was finished, she helped him put the cover back on. They stood back for a minute, observing for any confusion, any outright rejection of the new home. Daylight was rapidly fading, and it was getting difficult to see. Caleb touched her arm with his gloved hand.

"Come on. I think we've done all we can do here. It looks like the're settling in."

She now had eight hives. She felt a tiny prick in her heart at the awareness that she wanted to tell Corrie. She wanted to talk about the miracle of it all.

Caleb removed his hood as they started up the hill and she followed suit. Anna, straggling behind, remained fully clad. Caleb's phone buzzed in his pocket and he dug it out. "It's mom. I better see what she wants." He hit the screen and lifted the phone to his ear. "Hey, love of my life. What's up?"

She could hear Bri's voice, muffled on the other end. "Umhmm. Did you try turning on the breakers? Yeah, I know, mom, that's why I labeled them last summer." Bri's response was a little sharper, a little louder. "All right, all right. Don't worry. I'll handle it. I can be there in five minutes. ... It's okay. No worries. See you in a bit."

He closed his phone and turned to her and Anna, who had caught up by then. "Mom is having some electrical problems. She can't get the lights in her bedroom and bath to come on. She said she thinks she may have blown the circuit when she was using her stand mixer earlier today. I've shown her a million times how to flip those breakers, but she can't seem to remember." He smiled a lopsided grin. "It may be a ruse to get a prodigal son to come visit. I haven't been over to the farm for awhile. Sorry, ladies. Looks like you'll have to have dinner without me. Mom has some beans and cornbread she wants to share."

The thought of tripped breakers and blown circuits sobered her a little bit. Where was her breaker box, anyway? And were all the switches labeled? She would have to check that tomorrow. Oh, the joys of the single life. "Don't think a thing about it, Caleb. I can pack you up a pint of chili to go if you like. I made enough to send some home with you both."

"I'd never say no to your chili!" He turned to Anna. "Will you be okay here for a couple hours? Or you can come with me if you want but I figure you'll have a better time here. Better food too." He threw a grin her way.

Anna was still wearing her veil. "Ummm. I think I'll stay here and visit while you tend your mom. She might like to have you to herself for a bit. Just text me before you leave and pick me up on the way. Tell Bri hi."

"Will do." He leaned over to kiss Anna, but, faced with the hood, instead lifted her hand, turned it over, and delicately kissed the cup of it. "I'll be back to get you as soon as I get this all cleared up."

They had reached the porch by this time and both women watched Caleb climb into his truck and drive away before lumbering up the steps into the house. Scents of pepper and onion and simmering cumin drifted through the kitchen to meet them.

"The bowls are up here," she opened a cupboard door. "I have some tabasco, a little sharp cheddar, and some salted tortilla chips fresh out of the grease—" She flipped on the light switch just as Anna lifted the veil from her head. She stopped speaking when she looked at her dinner guest.

Anna's face was ashen, her lips a pale blue.

Anna smiled weakly at the expression on her face. "It's okay. I have an appointment with my cardiologist tomorrow."

"Anna! What does it mean? Are you okay? Please, sit down! What can I do?"

10

Anna set her hood on the table and lowered herself slowly into a chair. She fingered the snaps at the base of the hood, as she spoke.

"What does it *mean?*" Anna sighed and rubbed the hem of the hood with her thumb. "I was born with a heart condition called *truncus arteriosus.* What that means is where a normal heart has two separate main blood vessels leaving the heart—the aorta that carries blood to the body and the pulmonary artery that carries blood to the lungs—I only had one. The surgery I had when I was a baby involved inserting a conduit, or a valve, to separate my pulmonary artery from the main truncus—the vessel shared with the aorta.

"As I told you and Sarah before, I had to have that valve replaced once when I was young. I've been short of breath and easily winded for several days now. The symptoms I'm having might mean the valve is leaking, allowing too much blood flow into my lungs. I put off calling for a couple days, hoping I just had a little bug or something. But when it persisted, I knew I couldn't ignore it any longer. Dr. Janney worked me in as soon as she could. In the meantime, she prescribed me a medication to lower my blood pressure until she can do a thorough workup."

Anna stopped fiddling with the veil, looked up and met her eyes. Her lips were pinking up again, her skin regaining some color.

"What can *you* do? Will you go to my cardiologist appointment with me tomorrow? I know it's late notice but I—"

"Yes! Of course. Anna. Whatever you need."

Anna's eyes teared up and she looked away. "Thank you. I just...I don't want to be alone this time."

She sat down in the chair beside Anna and took her right hand. "Of course. It's no trouble at all, I don't have anything going on tomorrow. You tell me what time, and I'll pick you up."

Anna hesitated. "There's one more thing." She looked into her eyes again, pleading. "Please don't let Caleb know about this."

"Anna—"

"I haven't told him about my heart condition. I don't know why. I guess I just wanted a chance for him to grow to care about me. To get to know me. Not just the girl with the heart condition. To not be scared off by the possibility of—"

She squeezed Anna's hand.

"Anna, if you think something like this would scare Caleb Brown off, you don't know him very well."

"I know you are probably right. He's so good. And kind and decent. But if you only knew. So many times when I was a little girl I got my hopes up about being adopted—having a family of my own. But as soon as the potential adopters found out about my heart...*boom*. All that hope—shattered. I don't think...I just don't want to lose Caleb that way."

Tears were streaming down Anna's cheeks. She reached up and cupped Anna's chin, forced her to look into her eyes again.

"That is not going to happen. You hear me? People like me and Caleb, we don't abandon people when things get rough. We're stronger than that. You hear me? We know love is greater than pain. We know to love is to be afraid of losing. But it's worth it. You hear me?"

Anna's chin bobbed in her hand and they were both crying now. She reached over and wrapped her arms around the younger woman. "You just tell me the time and I'll be there."

~

I guess I hoped for
a single outcome,
water rushing
only my way
and somehow
not leaving
the others
high and dry

She sat with these words from Will Willingham, *Earth Song* open on her lap. Caleb had retrieved Anna hours ago, but she could not sleep. She kept rehearsing her words to her friend over and over in her mind.

We know love is greater than pain. We know to love is to be afraid of losing. But it's worth it. You hear me?

Did she really believe that? Could her heart really stand being broken again?

~

Dr. Janney's office was at Memorial Hospital, right in the center of town. The parking garage was nearly full; the only space she could find was on the south side of the eighth floor. As far away from the elevators as possible. She glanced at Anna's grim face.

"I should have dropped you off in the front. Do you want me to—"

"No, it's fine. I'll be okay."

She pulled into the spot, and they slowly made their way across the garage to the elevators. By the time they arrived at the waiting room, Anna's face was drained of all color and her breathing was shallow. The room was crowded but they found two seats near the registration desk. Anna slumped in her chair, exhausted. "Will you sign me in?" She asked, now one with the hard chair beneath her. The woman at the registration desk gave her the usual forms for Anna to fill out. As Anna mused over the questionnaires, she searched for the right words to comfort her young friend. Everything she tried out in her mind seemed ridiculous.

Finally, a woman in green scrubs appeared in the doorway, a wheelchair in front of her. "Anna Ferris?" she called, looking out into the sea of people. She helped Anna to her feet and the two of them made their way to the woman. Green Scrubs gestured for Anna to sit down in the wheelchair, but before they could do anything else she held up her hand and leaned in closer to Anna. "I'm so sorry, but your mom will have to wait here for now," she said quietly. "Dr. Janney has ordered a STAT MRI for you. We're going straight to radiology."

Anna turned quickly in the chair to look back at her, eyes wide, face drained of even more color. "Okay," she said, slowly, looking like she was about to cry. "But I need her with me when I see the doctor. Is that okay?"

Green Scrubs smiled and patted Anna's hand, which was white knuckling the clipboard containing her medical history. "Of course," she said. "I'll get her to you as soon as we're done with the MRI."

She reached out and squeezed Anna's shoulder before Green Scrubs whisked the girl through the door. It closed in her face with a solid click. She stared at its heavy wooden presence with a growing sense of dread, before quietly walking back to her seat to wait.

She read Li-Young Lee's poem "Degrees of Blue" three times and still could not focus on the words. It was this part she kept coming back to as she waited to be summoned back to Anna:

> *When he returns to the tale,*
> *the page is dark,*
>
> *and the leaves at the window have been traveling*
> *beside his silent reading*
> *as long as he can remember.*

How much longer?

She closed *Earth Song* and stretched her legs out from the uncomfortable chair. *Seriously. Do they make these chairs so hard on purpose? To discourage large numbers from waiting in the waiting room?* She looked around. The once full room was dwindling, all the people replaced by the suffocating presence of worry, worry, worry. She was steeling herself to approach the desk and inquire about Anna when Green Scrubs appeared in the magic doorway and beckoned her to follow. She stuffed *Earth Song* in her bag and hurried through the door with her escort.

She followed Green Scrubs down a long hall and was ushered through another heavy wooden door. There, she found Anna, clad in a paper gown, sitting on an exam table, face pale but somehow, still flushed and looking…happy?

Anna looked up at her with dewy eyes and a tremulous smile.

"I'm going to have a baby," she said. "I'm going to be a mama."

~

"Cardiac output increases by 30-50% during pregnancy. This happens early and usually plateaus between the second and third trimesters. Also, systemic vascular resistance decreases steadily until the end of the second trimester. And, due to the expansion in plasma volume, pregnant women experience physiologic anemia. All these factors contribute to increased flow, taxing your prosthetic valve."

Dr. Janney had a flipchart with illustrations of the human heart on the desk between her and them. She flipped over to an image of a heart following repair for *truncus arteriosus*. The doctor pointed to a prosthetic valve connecting the pulmonary artery to the right ventricle.

"Anna, the CT showed that your valve is still viable, but the changes in your body have caused some problems. There is not a lot of research out there on pregnancy following repair of *truncus arteriosus,* but what is out there indicates that with close medical management, outcomes are good. Most women experience a deterioration of valve regurgitation—

meaning valve leakage. This is why you are having the symptoms you've been having." She used a pen to trace up through the valve. "With a leaky valve, blood flows from the right ventricle out through the pulmonary artery and into the lungs—as it should — but some flows backwards into the right ventricle when the ventricle relaxes." She reversed her pen to show the backwards flow of blood. "Your heart is having to work harder to compensate for the blood leak back into the ventricle." She set the pen down on the desk. "We have some options for medical management, but you should know there are risks with pregnancy and heart valve disease—"

"What kind of risks?" Anna was sitting on the edge of her chair, carefully following everything the doctor said. Her right hand rested softly on her abdomen; her eyes studied Dr. Janney's face.

Dr. Janney met her eyes. "Preeclampsia, placental abruption, hemorrhaging, thrombosis, and—I'm being honest—increased mortality rates."

She felt Anna's body tense beside her, felt her own heartbeat quicken. She leaned forward and asked, "Doctor, what kind of percentage are we talking about here?"

Dr. Janney shifted her piercing gaze from Anna to her. She hesitated. "I'm afraid I don't have a good answer to that question. Most of what we know about this comes from case reports. And every case is highly individualized." She shifted her gaze back to Anna. "Anna, I know this must be very overwhelming for you. This is…a lot. You've been my patient a long time. I wish I could give you some time to absorb all this. Unfortunately, with the symptoms you're having, we need to make some decisions fairly quickly. I will email you some reading material later today. I'm going to have my staff set up an appointment for you with a colleague of mine who special- izes in cardiac obstetrics. He's hard to get in with, but he owes me a favor. And, Anna, you should know up front that should you choose to go through with this—"

"I am going through with this." Anna's gaze was unmoved.

Dr. Janney gave just a hint of a smile. "Okay. Well, you should know this will mean some pretty drastic life changes. We're talking bed rest, or something very close to it. You'll have to figure out a way to alter your workload. Maybe the university will let you teach remotely? Your dissertation re- search will have to wait. No more galavanting around the woods. We will have to closely monitor your blood pressure and likely use some medication management." She leaned in closer. "But if we stay on top of things and if you are a good patient, I think we can do this."

Dr. Janney scooted her chair out from behind the desk and headed toward the door. "I'll have my office staff call you later about your appointment time with the specialist. And Anna?" She glanced over her shoulder as she opened the door. "Maybe talk this over with the baby's father?"

The door closed behind her with a soft snap.

11

They drove back to her house in silence. Every time she opened her mouth to speak, she was quieted by a sidelong glance at Anna—who sat hunched in the passenger seat, staring out the side window. She pulled into the long driveway and swung the Subaru into the side car port. Wordlessly, they both got out of the car and climbed the porch steps. Anna dropped down into one of the patio chairs—the one Caleb always preferred—as if exhausted from the short walk from the car. A robin sang her slow, sweet song from some unseen, secret place.

She sat down in the porch swing and groped for words. "Tell me how I can help." It was all she could come up with.

Anna stared at nothing. "I don't know." She buried her face in her hands. "I don't know what to do. I don't know how I'm going to do this."

She reached over and touched Anna's arm. "We'll do it together. And Caleb—"

Anna abruptly lowered her hands from her face. "Caleb? I don't want Caleb to know anything about this!"

"Anna! You can't be serious." She rubbed Anna's arm where her hand rested. Silence. Then, "Give yourself some time to think about this. You don't have to decide everything all at once. Let's go inside. I'll brew a pot of green tea. We can make a list of what you need to do. Prioritize the logistical things. We'll figure out what I can do and what you need to take care of yourself."

Anna lifted her hand to the one rubbing her arm, squeezed fingers. Then she nodded and climbed to her feet.

Anna agreed to temporarily move into the farmhouse with her, knowing she'd need someone to drive her to appointments and be around...just in case. Any suggestion of Caleb's involvement was still adamantly opposed. How could one keep such a secret? She shook her head to herself. She'd been around long enough to know this wasn't her call to make. She hoped Anna would change her mind about that eventually.

She opened the top drawer of Anna's dresser and pulled out the flannel PJs requested, stacking them neatly in the suitcase open on the bed. Anna had drawn up a list of things she needed from her little cottage: clothes, her laptop, a box of research data, some class notes...fortunately, it was almost time for winter break, which made it easier to transition Anna's classes to another professor. Anna would finish out the semester teaching remotely and then go on sabbatical under the guise of working on her dissertation. Anna did not want anyone to know about her health situation, especially not the pregnancy.

"It's not entirely a lie," Anna had said. "If I'm on bed rest I'll need something to work on. I'll go crazy just laying around. My research trials are mostly finished. It won't be taxing to do the statistical analyses from a couch."

She'd asked about Anna's research then.

"I've been studying inoculating native orchid seedlings with mycorrhizal fungi in my lab. Most specifically Kentucky lady's slipper—*Cypripedium kentuckiense*. It takes three to five years to grow lady's slippers orchids from seed to flower, that's one reason it's taken me so long to pull all this research together. But if everything goes okay, they can live for hundreds of years! Anyway, it's difficult to grow some species of orchids in the laboratory and my results show the mycorrhizal fungi are key in overcoming this…" Anna looked up, cheeks flush. "Sorry. I get a little carried away…"

Um. Okay.

And thus, the next assignment. She zipped the suitcase and set it by the door before heading out to Anna's little greenhouse. As soon as she opened the door she was engulfed in moist heat. Hum of fans overhead and a quick check (as instructed) told her the thermostat was doing its job just fine. "Don't touch anything if you don't have to!" Anna had said. She was more than happy to comply.

She looked around at Anna's pretty workspace. She could see why her friend was loathe to leave this place. Breathing felt easier here. She inhaled deeply—a scent like jasmine, hint of mint, earthy and clean. Green everywhere. Giant leafy plants and small viny things curled around every vertical surface. Nothing blooming in early December, but it was wild, like a jungle. In the makeover ruse, Caleb had placed a custom-designed desk in one corner—so Anna could sit and record whatever she was working on for the day. In lieu of artwork, which could not tolerate the moist environment, he had used decorative tiles, metal work, and small sculptures throughout to give the wild a cultivated feeling.

She walked over to the workspace and found an open sketch book on the desktop. She flipped through watercolor washes of orchids and various other flowering plants. In the very back of the book was a rough sketch of Caleb, lopsided grin and all. The girl had it bad. Why in the world wouldn't she tell him the truth? She closed the book softly and looked around. Everything seemed fine. All of Anna's research was computerized. She was able to read the water and soil content levels of her orchids with an app connected to her laptop, so there was little work to be done here. Caleb had even installed a misting system to mimic rain forest levels of precipitation, so the plants did not require watering.

She took a quick picture with her phone and texted it to Anna. "Everything looks good here. Let me know if you think of anything else you need."

She frowned when she noticed she had one overlooked text. Tapping the screen she saw it was from Caleb.

"Is Anna with you? I've been texting her all day and she hasn't responded."

Great. How was she supposed to respond to that? She mulled over possible responses but couldn't figure out what to say without compromising her promise to Anna to keep her situation quiet for now. She pocketed the phone, deciding to ignore the message until she and Anna got their story straight.

She loaded the car up with all of Anna's requests, double checked the doors and windows were locked, and headed back home. She was thinking of how she would fix up the spare room for Anna. No one had slept in that bed for ages. She would need to wash the sheets when she got home. And find some fresh blankets. It could get chilly in there at night.

As she drove along, thinking, for some reason, the Jane Hirshfield poem, "Tree," she'd read that morning in *Earth Song* came suddenly to mind.

> *It is foolish*
> *to let a young redwood*
> *grow next to a house.*

The first stanza brought Anna's face to her mind's eye. Her life had always been calm...predictable. Until Corrie's illness. Even then they'd managed to keep a routine that allowed her to keep a semblance of order. But this...

> *Already the first branch-tips brush at the window.*
> *Softly, calmly, immensity taps at your life.*

Mulling over the poem's end left a lump in her throat.

Of all the ways love had wrecked her life, she could see it wasn't done with her yet. Briefly, she tried to muster a wall around her heart. But it was too late to protect herself from loving this young woman who would now live under her roof. Or the baby she carried inside her.

She sighed as she turned up the long drive, then startled as she realized Caleb's truck was parked by the porch.

Raised voices coming from inside the house. She lifted the suitcase from the backseat and headed to the front door. Caleb stormed out, slamming the screen door behind him.

"Caleb, what...?"

His cheeks were stained red, eyes burning. "I wish you'd warned me."

"Caleb..."

He held up his hand to silence her. "I'm done. Stupid fool that I am. I never saw it coming. But I...I learned a long time ago you can't make another person feel the same way you do."

He shook his head, rubbed his eyes redder, then he was gone.

She watched him drive away before carrying the suitcase through the door and setting it down by the table.

"Anna?"

Muffled sobs came from the back. She followed the sound through the back door, onto the covered porch. Anna was sitting on the chaise, tears streaming down her face.

"I told him I didn't love him," she said, white-faced. "I told him I didn't want to see him anymore." The last word was choked out by a sob.

"Oh, Anna." She went to her friend and put her arms around her. She held her until the tears subsided. Then she went and changed the bedclothes in the spare room.

12

She sat with Anna in the dimly lit room and waited for the ultrasound technician.

Thirty-two weeks.

That's how far they needed to get. On November 15—two days ago—when she saw Dr. Lowe, they calculated Anna was around 12 weeks pregnant. The optimal due date would be at the end of May, but Dr. Lowe was shooting for at least April 5.

"You're doing great!" he had assured a blue-lipped, shallow-breathing Anna when they were finally able to get in with the specialist. He adjusted the medications Dr. Janney had started her on only slightly. He gave her information to set up a patient portal where she could enter her blood pressure numbers three times a day. Along with that data, Anna would answer some other questions to keep the doctor abreast of how she was doing. He wanted her to continue following with Dr. Janney and keep weekly appointments with one of the general OBGYNs at his practice—a Dr. Pauley. Dr. Pauley would keep him informed of any concerns, along with the online portal information.

"Keep up the good work," he had said, patting Anna's shoulder as he handed her a stack of papers and opened the door of his office to usher them out.

Anna gave just a ghost of a smile at his praise—one of very few lately—and hunched up from the chair with mild effort. "Thank you, doctor," she had said, as they walked out the door. It wasn't until they got home that the nurse called about the ultrasound.

Anna had been on edge ever since.

"I know it's early, but I haven't felt any quickening yet. Shouldn't I have felt some movement by now? The moms on The Peanut site describe it feeling like butterflies. What if something's wrong with the baby's heart?" Anna had asked the ceiling yesterday morning when she brought her the morning breakfast tray.

"Then we'll deal with it," she'd replied, as she stirred honey into Anna's vitamin shake. Anna took the spoon from her fingers.

"I can do that," she'd said, a bit irritably.

Now, here they were. And Anna had been a bear all morning.

Earlier, she'd read W. S. Merwin's poem "Shadow Questions" in *Earth Song*.

> *How can so small a body*
> *cast such a long shadow*
> *The poet asks.*

She studied Anna's clenched jaw, furrowed brow. *Long shadow, indeed.* She wondered could Anna could stop worrying long enough to be able to dream of holding a baby in her arms?

The door opened and a young man in pink scrubs entered the small room.

"Good morning!" He almost sang, looking at the chart in his hands. "Ms. Ferris? I'm Rob, I'll be working with you this morning. How are we doing today?"

He set the chart down on the counter, removed a clean sheet from a cupboard, and unfolded it, shaking it out over Anna's lower self.

"We consumed large amounts of water this morning, as instructed, and we are in pain from an overfull bladder," Anna replied crossly.

Rob hesitated and then gathered the sheet back up in his arms. "I'm so sorry. That does tend to be a problem. Do you want to empty your bladder a wee bit before we begin? Not too much, just enough to take the edge off, okay?"

Anna grunted. "No. Let's just get this over with. I'll be fine."

All righty then. So this is how it was going to be.

Rob fluffed the sheet back over Anna. "You just let me know if you change your mind," he said, gently. "If you will, just pull your gown up over your baby bump so we can get started."

Anna shifted her gown up and Rob adjusted the sheet so her still slim abdomen was exposed. He squeezed some gel on her belly and Anna's sharp intake of breath told her the stuff was cold.

"Sorry bout that," Rob said. "Is this your first ultrasound?"

Anna nodded.

"You probably know that an ultrasound uses sound waves to create a picture of the baby in your womb. It's old tech, painless, and there are no known side-effects to you or your baby. We'll use this information to confirm your due date, make sure the development is where it should be and look for any red flags. We'll also get a good look at your uterus, placenta, and fallopian tubes to make sure there are no problems there. Dr. Pauley will go over the results with you as soon as we're done."

He smiled at Anna as he picked up the wand. "After you've emptied your bladder."

Anna just glared at him. Rob cleared his throat and glanced over at her. "Are you mom?"

She smiled at him. *Poor guy.* "No, I'm just a friend. Anna is staying with me during the pregnancy. I'm sure you know her history. She's been worried about the baby's heart. Will we be able to see it at this point?"

Rob placed the wand on Anna's abdomen and started moving it around slowly, staring at the sonogram screen. "A little pressure," he said. "Um—we definitely will get a good listen to the heartbeat. The heart chambers won't be developed enough to really see until between 17-20 weeks. With your history, Anna, Dr. Pauley might order a fetal echocardiogram between the 18-20 week mark somewhere. Right now, we will make sure the heart rate is normal."

The room fell silent except for a swishing sound emitting from the machine.

"Let's see," Rob said, almost to himself. He clicked a few buttons on the screen. "Placenta looks good." More swishing and clicking. "Everything checks out with your uterus! You have good anatomy!"

"Um, thanks?" Anna said dryly. Rob shifted on his stool.

"Let's see if we can get a good look at this little one."

Anna turned her face away from the screen.

"Here we are," Rob said. She couldn't make out much in that sea of black and white on the screen. She leaned in closer.

"Let me take some measurements and then I'll try to give you a closer look."

More clicking and swishing. "There! Okay, now for the fun part."

Anna's face remained turned to the wall.

"Here we have a tiny profile. What do you think, mom?"

Rob smiled Anna's way. Until he saw her averted face.

"Anna." She touched her friend's arm. "Don't you want to see?"

She watched Anna's throat bob. "I don't think so. I don't want to…I need to hear the heart first."

How can so small a body
cast such a long shadow

"Ah." Rob studied the back of Anna's head for a second. "I can do that." He adjusted the wand, studying the screen, hit a couple buttons. "Hmm. Let's see."

Anna sniffed.

She held her breath.

Suddenly the room was filled with a swishing heartbeat, rapid but strong.

Anna slowly turned her head to look at the screen. "Is it …is it okay?" She asked, quietly.

"Yes," Rob said. "It sounds perfect."

He moved the wand around again until the tiny, fuzzy profile appeared on the monitor again. He quickly tapped a button and a small printout scrolled out. Rob plucked up the picture and handed it to Anna.

Anna studied the image in her hand, tears rolling down

her cheeks. "Thank you," she whispered. "Thank you."

13

Anna would not stay in bed. She limited her travels from the back porch to the kitchen table to her bedroom. Sometimes she visited the front porch. But she was wary of Caleb driving by and besides, they were full into winter now, so she mostly kept inside.

She was a caged animal. Wild.

"I've run and re-run the data a million times! A person can only do so many multi-variate analyses. I'm stuck right here until I can start the next batch of orchids. It's so frustrating!"

"Anna."

"I wish I could go over to my greenhouse. Just for a few hours. My numbers have been good. Maybe Dr. Lowe is being overcautious. I think it would—"

"Anna."

"—be good for my spirits to get my fingers in the dirt. I can be careful. Wear that portable heart monitor…"

She walked over to the fridge as Anna made her case. Removed the black and white image from the magnet. Strode over to Anna and placed the slip of square paper in her hand. Anna stopped talking and studied the shadow profile in the picture. A soft smile tugged at the corners of her lips.

"Are you willing to take that risk?"

Anna looked up at her and slowly shook her head. Then she looked back at the thin scrap of paper in her hand. A different door to walk through. "I'm just so dag-gone stir-crazy."

They had made it through Thanksgiving. Anna was six-teen weeks pregnant—four weeks into the second trimester. Sixteen weeks. Half-way there. Christmas was two weeks away and the only other person who knew Anna was pregnant was her sister, Aida. The two women talked on the phone every day, but after her wedding Aida had moved to Dallas with her new husband. Fifteen hundred miles and a lifetime away. She'd never asked Anna how much Aida knew, but she had a suspicion that the younger girl had no idea how risky the pregnancy was.

Sarah knew Anna had moved into the farm, but Anna had asked her to wait a little while to reveal she was pregnant. She didn't want her friend to have to lie to Caleb if they ran into each other.

And Anna still refused to tell Caleb.

He had called Anna a few times, but she would never an-swer. *If only I could find a way to get them to talk,* she thought. She didn't even think Caleb knew Anna was staying with her. Since it wasn't mowing season, there was no reason for he and June to stop by. She assumed they were busy with the snowplow-ing part of their business this time of year. Then she had a thought.

"Anna, you know, Caleb could help me put together a tabletop greenhouse. We could put it out on the sun porch, and I could fetch your seedlings and samples from your place. That way you could keep working on your research without much physical activity. He won't even have to know it's for you. I can tell him I'm experimenting with some stuff for the garden. Why don't I call him?"

At the mention of Caleb's name Anna had grown very

still. A cloud veiled her eyes and her brow furrowed. She knew the possibility of continuing her research would be very tempting for this restless animal living under her roof. "I don't know…" Anna hesitated. "I hate to ask you to lie for me."

"I can plant some of my own things too. That way I wouldn't be lying."

"But I'll have to hide while he's here."

"That's not a big deal. We'll tuck you in to the back room with a good book."

Anna chewed her lower lip. "It would be so nice to have something useful to work on. Are you sure you don't mind?"

She couldn't help herself. "Are you sure you won't just tell him, Anna? Do you think it's fair to keep this from him? He may not forgive you when he finds out the truth."

Anna braced her arms on the table and pushed herself up from her chair. "I should have known this was a trick."

"This was not a trick, Anna. I just don't understand. How can you do this to Caleb?"

Anna's eyes flashed. "I'm trying to protect him! If—if I don't make it through this, or the—the baby doesn't…don't you understand? I don't want to hurt him! You, of all people should understand what I'm trying to protect him from!"

Now it was her turn to grow still. The empty place in her heart gave a thump and she felt her eyes stinging. "Yes," she said, her voice raspy, barely able to speak. "I do understand. I do know what it feels like to lose someone you love. But I wouldn't trade one second of the time Corrie and I had together. Even if I'd known how it would end. The grief, the joy…in the end, it's all the same thing. Love. I wouldn't trade a second. And call me crazy, but I believe Caleb would feel the same way."

Anna closed her eyes. "I'm sorry." Her voice was barely a whisper. "I know. I just can't face it right now. It's taking everything in me just to keep going for us," she gestured to her belly. "I will tell him, I promise. I just want to wait until I'm further along. When it's safer."

She shook her head and saw Anna panting and the blue creeping around her lips again. She sprang into action. "Calm down, sweetheart. Here, let me help you," she said, as she moved over and wrapped her arms around the girl, helping Anna lower herself back down in the chair. "I'll get the blood pressure cuff."

And that was the end of that discussion.

Despite their argument, she called Caleb.

"I heard Anna is staying with you."

"Yes. She's been helping me with Little Indigo and I asked her to move in for a little while. It's just easier. Only temporary. She hasn't given up her cottage."

It was the story they'd agreed upon. So much for not lying.

"Well, I don't know if I'm ready to see her yet. I don't know how I feel about…"

"She won't be here. Don't worry. We'll plan it for a time when she's out." More lies.

There was silence on the other end. Then, "Okay. I'm glad to help. I'll order the greenhouse kit from my supplier. It'll take a couple weeks to come in. I'll call you when it arrives, and we'll plan from there."

"Thank you, Caleb, you are a peach."

"That's what they tell me."

She hung up the phone and gave a silent plea to the universe that this plan would work.

~

"But do I want to know the sex of the baby?"

Anna was hunched down in the passenger's seat, wrapped in layers—down-filled puffy coat, red toboggan with a fluffy ball on top, voluminous scarf that Aida had knitted for her for Christmas. It was cold outside. The little Subaru couldn't warm up fast enough.

They were at twenty weeks. Twenty weeks and this was a makeup ultrasound. The last ultrasound—the first one where it would have been possible to tell the gender—had been canceled due to the huge snowstorm that struck the night before. The same snowstorm that prevented Caleb from keeping their greenhouse assembly date. The same snowstorm that kept him so busy with snow removal that they may never get to assemble the darn thing. And therefore, Anna still wasn't any closer to telling him her secret.

"I can't answer that for you," she said, eyes trained to the road, scanning for black ice. "But if you don't," she dared a glance over to her side, "is it okay if they tell me? Because I WANT TO KNOW!"

Anna playfully punched her in the side. "There's no way you could keep a secret. So. NO. WAY."

"Oh, come on! I most definitely can keep a secret. But if you won't let me know until you know then I think you do want to know, if you're really asking me." She stopped laughing abruptly. "Unless…"

"Unless what?" Anna was smiling.

She glanced nervously at her friend. "Unless you want to wait until you tell Caleb and the two of you find out together," she said. Very quietly.

Anna did not respond right away. She studied the white road in front of them, the white sky above. "I'm still not ready for that yet. Okay?"

She sighed. "Okay." What could she say?

~

They pinned the ultrasound picture up on the fridge, next to the two before. There was a little arrow pointing to a tiny piece of the image. "Boy parts," it said. She squinted to read the small scribble in the white frame around the image: *Rowan.*

Anna's father's name.

14

Twenty-six weeks.

They fell into a quiet routine. Weekly appointments with Dr. Pauley. Bi-weekly with Dr. Lowe. Ultra-sounds every four weeks. Anna had finally started showing, but still struggled to gain weight. Dr. Lowe said Rowen was developing well, it was Anna who was suffering. Her cardiac output declined with each appointment. She was sleeping most of the day now—all thoughts of research a memory.

Which was a good thing, because her plan to get Anna to talk to Caleb was pretty much dead-in-the-water. Or in-the-snow, more like. Caleb had dropped the greenhouse kit off weeks ago, but he'd been unable to clear his schedule to assemble the thing. The giant box sat like an eye-sore on the back patio—a constant reminder of her failure. Anna avoided looking at it when she managed to leave her room and wander about the house. Today was one of those days. Anna sat glumly at the kitchen table, pushing scrambled eggs around her plate with her fork.

"What does your week look like?" Anna asked, weakly.

It was their standard way of greeting the morning. She gave Anna a run-down of her catering gigs, then they went over the scheduled medical appointments. She ran some water over the dishes in the sink. "It's a slow week. I have that Valentine luncheon down at the senior center on Wednesday. That's all. I've already gotten the ingredients for the tarts and donuts. I'll put everything together tomorrow night."

Anna grimaced, rubbing her side. "Rowan is very squirmy this morning," she drew a sharp intake of breath, then closed her eyes and started taking slow, deliberate breaths. In and out. In and out.

"Are you okay?" She dried her hands with a towel and grabbed the blood pressure cuff from its usual place on the counter. Anna waved her off.

"I'm fine. I just...ooh! He's just never been such a hard hitter before." She arched her back, still massaging her side.

Before she could insist they check Anna's blood pressure, they heard a car turn into the driveway. She peeked out the window and saw Caleb's truck moving toward the house.

"It's Caleb!"

Anna stood up too abruptly and, off balance, plopped back down in the chair. "Help me get to the back bedroom!" She offered Anna her arm and together they made it to the bedroom door before a loud knock sounded through the house. Anna said, "Go! I'll be fine." She opened the door and lowered herself onto the bed.

Closing the door behind her, she took a deep breath and headed to the front door.

"Caleb! What a nice surprise! Come in, before you freeze us both to death!" He ducked through the door, removing his gloves and toboggan.

"I was down this way checking on mom and thought I'd stop in to see if you need anything. I can't stay long; I have two teams out on different jobs and I need to get over to the high school to handle some things there..."

"Oh, sweetheart, you shouldn't have bothered with me. I'm just fine. My old Subaru goes like a plow through the snow. This weather hasn't slowed me down at all. Coffee?" She held up the pot and raised her eyebrows.

Caleb smiled. "Sure. I always have time for a cuppa with you." His sharp eyes roved around the kitchen, pausing on the half-eaten plate of scrambled eggs, the blood-pressure cuff. He turned slowly and looked out through the screened porch. "I'm sorry about that greenhouse project. I might be able to get to it next week. I think if you get some seeds started before the first of March it still might be useful."

She poured coffee into a mug and held it out to him. "No worries," she said. "I know how busy you've been. Cream's in the fridge."

"I do believe I'll have some today." He took the mug and moved over to the refrigerator. She shined the counter with a dishcloth. Caleb reached to open the fridge but stopped abruptly. When she realized what he was looking at, it was too late. "Is Sarah pregnant?" he asked, studying the checkerboard quilt of ultrasound pictures decorating the front of the icebox.

A strange noise came from her throat, but she couldn't seem to form any words. She saw the understanding slowly dawn over his face. Caleb reached out and plucked the latest ultrasound photo from the fridge. She knew Anna's name was in the lower left corner. He turned to her slowly, his face a cloud of confusion, hurt, and anger.

"What in the name of the holy hound is going on here?"

Before she could respond, the door to the back bedroom flew open and Anna fell through. She was on her hands and knees when they both sprang to her side. "S-something is wrong. It's still too early," she said, collapsing onto her back. Caleb caught her upper body and cradled her in his arms.

"Caleb?" Anna looked up into Caleb's eyes, lifted her hand and cupped his jaw. "Take care of Rowan." Then she started convulsing.

"Call an ambulance!" Caleb shouted, and she already had her phone in her hand, punching the numbers. She felt the cold grip of fear squeeze her heart and tears rolled heavily down her cheeks as she watched Caleb shelter Anna's body, being especially protective of the place where his baby dwelt.

15

Nothing. *Nothing* she'd ever seen prepared her to see Anna's body like that. Not the slow, wasting away of Corrie's body to the cancer. Not the heavy-lidded sleepiness induced by medication and pain. Not the hallucinations or confusion that came near the end. The image of Anna writhing uncontrollably was a horror that sat in the pit of her stomach, at the back of her throat, pressed in on the base of her brain, replaying over and over.

At least Caleb had been with her in the ambulance. The paramedics tried to prevent him, but when she shouted he was the baby's father, they relented. He clambered through the double doors of the vehicle and sat down by Anna's still figure, medics attaching her to tubes and wires, his eyes dark with confusion and fear. His found hers, a million questions brimming, before the doors closed with a bang. She ran to the Subaru and followed the vehicle as closely as she could, flashers on.

The baby was in distress, they were told. Anna had left Advance Directives: Rowan came first. She was undergoing an emergency C-section now. A surgical nurse explained it all to them as Dr. Lowe prepped for the surgery. Anna had to be intubated, had gone into cardiac arrest shortly after arriving at the ER. She would be on a heart monitor during the surgery. All precautions would be taken. The hope was that once Rowan was delivered, Anna's heart would recover, and no additional surgery would be required.

That was the hope.

But they were given all kinds of cautionary tales as well. Anna was sedated. Time would tell if she would awaken on her own. If the damage to the valve was too severe…If they hadn't waited too long…If her heart was strong enough…

As the nurse continued talking, she began to feel she could not breathe. And she couldn't still the shaking inside her. Caleb, as if sensing her rising panic, reached over and took her hand in his. The steadiness of his calloused fingers calmed her racing heart and brought tears of gratitude to her eyes.

The nurse's warm brown eyes held hers. "Dr. Lowe is an amazing surgeon. The cardiac team is standing by. Dr. Janney is on call. Anna is in good hands," she said, gently, before excusing herself.

They sat in tense silence. Caleb was so quiet. She thought of the end of the Wendell Berry poem she'd read in *Earth Song* the other day.

> *Accept what comes from silence.*
> *Make the best you can of it.*
> *Of the little words that come*
> *out of the silence, like prayers*
> *prayed back to the one who prays,*
> *make a poem that does not disturb*
> *the silence from which it came.*

She accepted the silence, closing her eyes like a prayer. But then a thought struck her.

"I had better call Aida," she said, reaching into her purse for her phone. Caleb stiffened beside her.

"Aida knew about this?"

She swallowed. "Yes. She knew Anna was pregnant. I don't think…she knew…how dangerous it was."

Caleb stood up abruptly and paced to the other side of the room.

"Caleb–"

"I don't understand," he said, clenching and unclenching his fists. "How could she keep this from me?"

She sighed. "She thought she was protecting you. She was going to tell you, Caleb. I promise. She just wanted to wait until she was further along. Until the baby was safe. This is exactly what she was afraid of happening. Her heart condition…"

He turned his head sharply to look at her. "Her *heart* condition? All those months we were together. She never told me anything about her heart. She told me about losing her parents. About growing up an orphan. But not that. Why? Why didn't she trust me with that?"

"I-I don't know if I understand it enough to explain. Except that she has lost so much in her short life. It made her afraid, I think? She wanted you to love her for who she was— who she was besides the heart condition. It was…she said it was the reason she was never adopted. It scared too many people off. I tried to tell her you aren't like that, Caleb. She knew you weren't. I think…I think she just wanted to pretend she was like anyone else. You made her want that to be true."

He sat down in a chair across from her and buried his face in his hands, exhaling deeply. "It wouldn't have mattered to me," he said, through his fingers. "I was—I am—crazy about her."

He lifted his head, those blue eyes piercing through her.

"I can't lose her now."

Before she could respond, Dr. Lowe walked into the room. They both stood up when they saw him. He smiled weakly at them both, removing his surgical cap as he drew near. "Everything went well," he said, and she let out a long breath she hadn't realized she was holding. "Anna's been transferred to telemetry. She'll undergo an MRI shortly to get a good look at that valve. She's still sedated, of course, so we don't know..." He hesitated.

If she'll wake up. If she'll ever get to hold her son. If I will ever hear her laugh again.

"Well, we need a little time to see how she recovers."

She wobbled a little on her feet. Caleb reached out an arm to steady her and turned to Dr. Lowe.

"The baby?"

Dr. Lowe smiled. "He seems to be doing fine. He's breathing on his own. His heart looks good. There are...risks to being born so early, but we will talk about those later. He's undergoing some initial tests, but that shouldn't take too long. Would you like to meet your son?"

16

He was so small. Twenty-seven ounces, to be exact. Just a little over a pound and a half. She watched the nurse demonstrate to Caleb how to reach through a hole in the incubator and gently touch his child.

"His skin is fragile, so, no stroking. Just gently lay your fingers here," she rested her hand lightly on Rowan's leg. "Or here." Moved up to his arm. "Some parents like to touch their baby's face," she lightly touched a finger to a cheek. "Or their heads."

Caleb leaned in close, never taking his eyes off his son, the yellow hospital gown he wore over his work clothes making a soft crinkling sound as he shifted. The nurse pulled her hand out of the incubator and nodded to him to take her place. He swallowed and shifted his eyes to hers.

"Are you sure it's okay? My hands are so much bigger than yours. What if I—"

She touched his arm reassuringly. "It's perfectly safe, as long as you are gentle—the way I showed you. In fact, it's best for Rowan." She bent down and looked Caleb in the eye. "He needs to feel human touch. It's essential for his thriving."

Caleb nodded, throat bobbing again, and slowly extended his hand into the incubator. She watched, tears welling, heart swelling. This tiny life. Attached to so many wires and tubes. So still and quiet…

"Caleb, wait!" she said, through tears. "Let me take a picture. Anna will…" she swallowed hard. "Anna will want to see the first time you met Rowan." She pulled her phone out of her pocket and pointed it their way.

Caleb didn't even shift his gaze. He was slowly inching his fingers toward Rowan's leg. He rested a finger on a tiny shin, curled the palm of his hand around Rowan's foot. "Hey, there, buddy," he whispered. "Hey, Rowan. It's me, your...your daddy." He moved his finger up to touch the baby's cheek. When he rested his finger on the curve of his son's face, Rowan startled in response, lifting his tiny arms and legs all at once before settling back down. Caleb withdrew his hand and gave the nurse beside him a questioning look.

"It's okay. That's good. He's responding well to your touch. Rowan is strong. He has good lungs," she smiled at Rowan's pinking face crumpling as he made an effort to elicit a soundless cry. "Keep talking to him. At this stage in development, his hearing should be fully functional. When he gets a little stronger, we will do some kangaroo care—let you hold him, skin to skin—in an upright position on your chest."

Caleb nodded; eyes once again rapt on his son. He reached back inside to touch Rowan's arm. "Hey, little guy," he said, softly. "It's going to be okay; you hear me? You don't have to worry about a thing. Just growing and getting stronger. That's your job right now. Your mommy is going to be so smitten with you when she meets you. She'll be here soon. Save up some good stuff for her. But until she comes, I'm going to be here. Okay? We're going to get to know each other very well. You're going to be okay. You're a fighter, I can tell. Just like your mama."

Caleb turned his wet eyes to hers. She nodded. *Yes. It was going to be okay. It had to be.*

Just then, Dr. Janney walked through the NICU door. She looked tired and frazzled, a surgical cap still on her head. "I need to talk with the two of you," she said.

Caleb withdrew his hand from the incubator and stood up. Dr. Janney pierced him with the intensity of her gaze. "We're having trouble getting Anna to wake up. We need to talk about what that might mean."

17

On the third day of Anna's deep sleep, Aida flew in to be with her sister. And meet her nephew. She picked Aida up at the airport and tried not to be distracted by the way the girl's brow furrowed just like her sister's when she was troubled. On the short drive to the hospital Aida had peppered her with questions. She'd answered as best as she could, but her brain was so addled from splitting her days and nights between Anna and Rowan, that Aida seemed less than satisfied.

No, Anna was not opening her eyes at all yet.

No, she did not respond in any visible way to external stimuli.

No, the doctors did not know why she wouldn't wake up.

Yes, her heart was functioning normally again. She was being fed through a tube inserted into her nose down into her stomach.

Yes, she was permitted to stay the night with her sister, but only one person at a time could do so. And Caleb. He had insisted on being there most nights.

Yes, Rowan was doing very well, had even gained a couple ounces.

"The doctors have encouraged us to provide gentle stimulation to, you know, wake up parts of her brain, maybe. I've been doing a little aroma therapy with essential oils. And I like to bring in some of her favorite aromatic foods. She loved those peach tarts we made for your wedding shower so much." She paused at the memory and was surprised to feel her eyes moisten. "Bri—Caleb's mom—made some yesterday and dropped them by. We let her get a good inhale. Caleb brought some of her favorite music. And he gives her massages every morning and evening—rubs her arms and legs, around her temples and jaw. We've been taking it in turns to stay with her or Rowan. Caleb is doing the kangaroo care with Rowan now—holding him skin to skin." She glanced over at Aida's furrowed brow. "He really is beautiful…" Her voice choked up as an image of little man came to her mind's eye.

Aida reached over and rubbed her arm, her eyes welling too. "I can't wait to meet him." She swallowed. "It's all been so hard for me to wrap my mind around. Anna never told me about the risks. I should have known. But I guess I was just so …so wrapped up in being married. So wrapped up in Greg. If I had known…I would have been here. I should have known…"

"Hey." Her turn to reach over and pat Aida's leg, keeping her eyes on the road. "Of course you were, with very good reason. Every new bride deserves to be. I'm sure that's why Anna didn't burden you with the risks. She didn't want to ruin your first days together."

Aida gave her a watery smile. "I just wish I had been here. She's always been here for me. And Anna…Anna got the worst end of the deal in too many ways. I wanted this to be the happy ending."

She sighed. "I know what you mean." She glanced Aida's way. "But you're here now. And I know Anna will be glad."

They went to Anna's room first. Caleb must have been with Rowan, or taking a break, because the room was empty and silent except for the beeps of monitors and soft music playing at Anna's bedside. Aida sat down in the chair by the head of the bed. She smoothed her sister's hair behind her ear, careful not to pull the feeding tube. Her lips trembled as she bent to kiss Anna's cheek.

"Hello, beautiful," she said, softly. "I'm here. I'm not leaving until you wake up." Fat tears rolled down her cheeks. They sat together for an hour, Aida humming softly to her sister as she gave her a manicure. "What do you think?" Aida asked, pulling two bottles of nail lacquer from her purse. "Clear? Red? Or," she rummaged around further in the large satchel, "purple?" she said, pulling another bottle out.

"Definitely purple," said a voice from the doorway.

Aida looked up. She shifted uncomfortably in her seat. "Hello, Caleb."

They hadn't seen each other since the wedding, but Caleb blanched visibly at her cool tone.

Aida went on, shifting her eyes from Caleb to her sister's still face. "Thanks for helping with Anna. But I'm here now. You don't need to trouble yourself further."

The shock on Caleb's face was palpable. "What?"

Aida looked up at him. "Anna told me about the breakup. She would be so angry with me if I let you take care of her out of pity."

What had Anna told the girl?

She watched Caleb struggle to maintain composure. "So. Anna told you all the details of our breakup, did she?"

Aida shrugged. "She didn't have to. It didn't take a genius to see how much you'd hurt her. When every time I mentioned your name, she started to cry and refused to speak about it."

"Aida, honey…" she started to explain.

"I'm going to check on Rowan," Caleb interrupted, and he was gone.

When the door clicked closed behind him, she picked up

a chair by the door and moved it over close to Aida. The girl was scared. She knew that sometimes, when difficult things happen, some people need a scapegoat. She couldn't let Aida blame Caleb unfairly. Not for anything. She reached out and took Aida's hands.

"Hey," she said, as gently as she could. "There are some things you need to know." Then she told Aida. Everything.

When she was done, they were both crying. "I hate this," Aida said. "Why did she think she had to go through this all alone?"

"Well," she said, softly, "she did have me."

Aida wrapped her in her arms and buried her face in her shoulder. "Yes. Yes she did. I'm so grateful. She loves you so much. Did you know that?" Aida held her at arm's length and studied her face as she asked the question.

She smiled weakly. "Yes, I guess I do. And I love her."

Aida dropped her arms. "It looks like my sister has found the family she's always wanted."

They held each other's gaze, smiling. Then Aida wiped her eyes. "Will you show me where I can find Rowan? I want to meet my nephew. And I owe Caleb an apology."

As they drew near the NICU, her fingers were itching to touch her little man. But only two were allowed to visit at once and she could see Caleb, gowned up, fingers resting on his son's leg. The nurse helped Aida put on her yellow gown and mask and she watched through the window as Aida approached the incubator. Caleb was still as Aida approached, one finger gently tapping Rowan's right foot. She couldn't hear what was said, but as Aida studied Rowan's tiny figure, she suddenly crumpled, bent over with shaking sobs. Caleb slowly withdrew his hand from his son's leg and went to her. He held her in his arms as Aida wept.

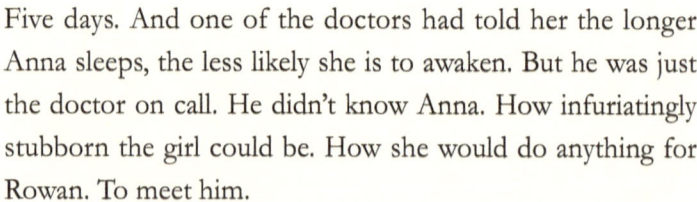

18

Five days. And one of the doctors had told her the longer Anna sleeps, the less likely she is to awaken. But he was just the doctor on call. He didn't know Anna. How infuriatingly stubborn the girl could be. How she would do anything for Rowan. To meet him.

She kept playing the videos she'd taken of the baby every time she visited Anna. But Rowan was so quiet, still too weak to cry out very much. So she would give an oral narrative.

"Rowan loves when I tickle the bottoms of his feet. See how he looks at me when I do? I swear, I think he's smiling. He makes these little chirping noises when he's happy. I think he might have Caleb's eyes. I thought you'd like that. Remember how you used to go on about his eyes? Besotted. That's what you were. All the other babes in the NICU have these milky blue eyes, but not our Rowan. Nope, his eyes are deep blue—like the sea. And so clear. When I sing to him, he goes real still, like he's listening so hard. But really, it's too early to tell. About his eyes, I mean. He sleeps a lot, which the nurse says is normal, so we don't get to see his baby blues very often. But when he does open his eyes…oceans. Caleb says he has your lips—which I can see…"

Honestly, she'd never talked so much in her whole life. She'd prattle on about anything and everything, studying Anna's face for so much as an eyelash flutter. Nothing was working.

~

She sighed and looked around the greenhouse. She was still stopping by Anna's cottage every few days to make sure the plants were behaving. Everything was doing well with the auto-watering system Caleb had installed. She spent a few minutes in boring conversation with a pitcher plant (as Anna had once instructed her, "Let them get used to your voice. I know they must be missing mine."). She was speculating on something she could take to the hospital to share with Anna. But they had already moved all the individually potted orchids over to her house. That's what she would do—stop at the house and pick up one of Anna's beloved orchids. She took one last look around and hurried out.

She hadn't been home since Anna's collapse. It felt like another lifetime ago. She stood still in the kitchen, taking in the dirty dishes on the table, half-filled cup of coffee abandoned on the counter. She tried to block out the image of Anna, falling to the floor, body convulsing in Caleb's arms. She grabbed her kitchen smock and moved over to the table, picked up the plate of dried out scrambled eggs—scraped them into the trash bin and ran a sink of hot, soapy water. She felt tension move up through her back, along her cervical spine and down through her arms and fingers. With each dish dipped and cleaned she felt her body relax further, until she wiped her hands on her apron and looked up out over the back yard.

She was surprised to see Corrie's daffodils blooming. *Was it spring already?* She untied the apron and found herself in the back yard, inspecting the green fingers of other bulbs pointing up through the earth. There were still piles of dirty snow along the edges of the street out front but a sudden snap of warm had awakened these beauties almost overnight.

She wondered about the bees.

She glanced at her phone to gauge the time, deleted the notification for the usual eleven o'clock phone call, closing her eyes as she did so. She had just enough time to walk down the hill and lay eyes on the hives. Aida was going to visit her parents today, so she would need to be quick to pick up an extra shift sitting with Anna.

In the apiary grove she stopped a short distance from the hives. She was close enough to see the honeybees stirring. She watched each hive in turn, just long enough to see foragers coming and going from each one. She knew she should do a more thorough inspection soon to make sure they'd all made it through the winter unscathed. She felt a twinge of guilt. Maybe she needed to tell Rhoda to take the bees.

She mused as she watched the tiny shadows flit around the hives. "Oh, Corrie…"

How could she take care of these honeybees *and* take care of Anna? Despite the heaviness of that thought, something about the bustling bees made her feel hopeful. She felt lighter as she made her way back up the hill, gathering an armful of daffodils from the multitudes Corrie had planted along the banks. Their earthy perfume might be more stimulating than the more subdued fragrance of Anna's orchid collection. Back in her kitchen, she wrapped the flowers in wax paper and grabbed a colorful plastic oversized cup from the cabinet to use as a makeshift vase. She'd fill it with water when she got there. Hurrying, she grabbed a light jacket, the daffodils, and was on her way.

Aida was still at Anna's bedside when she arrived. She glanced at the younger woman as she filled the cup-vase from the sink. "Any news?"

Aida shook her head. There were dark circles marring the delicate skin under her eyes. Aida stood up and stretched as she unwrapped the daffodils from the wax paper.

"Those are cheerful," Aida said, the glum note of her voice anything but. Just then, something buzzed out of the bouquet of flowers. Both women flinched as a tiny, winged creature flitted maniacally up to the light, then back down and over to the window.

"What is it?" Aida asked, rolling up the newspaper that had been idling on the bedside table.

"I'm not sure," she responded, as the creature flew over their heads and neared Anna's bed. Aida prepared to strike with her homemade swatter. The creature seemed to hover in the air above Anna's sleeping face and then slowly descended. Wait. Was it? "Aida, wait!"

The two stood frozen, not daring to breathe, as the tiny honeybee landed on Anna's cheek and began to crawl across the hollows of her face.

"But what if it stings her?" Aida's eyes were wide.

"Don't frighten it and it won't." She moved closer and bent in to study the bee.

The honeybee was crawling up the bridge of Anna's nose. Every few steps it would stop and wiggle its antenna, rub its legs together, lower its proboscis as if tasting Anna's skin. She could see two yellow balls of pollen collected on each of the bee's hind legs.

The bee continued her journey across the terrain of Anna's face. She crawled over Anna's right eye, stopped mid lid, lowered her head and seemed to touch her mouth to Anna's eyelid. They watched in astonishment as the bee lifted herself in flight and landed on Anna's other eyelid and did the same thing.

Aida caught her eye. "What is happening?"

She did not dare speak as the honeybee then flitted to Anna's mouth and landed. There was a turning around, almost a twirl, and she recognized the dance that honeybees will do to communicate to their co-workers where a good patch of nectar might be. The bee touched her face to Anna's lips—a honeybee kiss—hesitated briefly, and then lifted herself back into the air. She followed the bee to the window and, as if heeding a silent request, opened it a crack. The honeybee flew out and disappeared into the sky. She was looking after it when she heard Aida make a strange sound.

She turned from the window to see Anna, eyes open, blinking. She rushed over to the side of the bed and grabbed Anna's hand, searched her face. There were tiny yellow granules of pollen on her lips. Anna licked her top lip and asked, "Where is Rowan?"

19

She'd just put Rowan down in the bassinet for his morning nap when the phone buzzed at the usual time. She stared at the name on the screen.

Ballard Monument Co.

To her surprise, she watched her finger accept the call. It felt like that digit belonged to someone else and wasn't attached to her body.

"Hello?" she said, her voice sounding hollow to her own ears.

"Ah, um, hello! I wasn't expecting someone to answer. I've been calling for weeks now and would have given up long ago if Frank didn't insist I keep trying…"

"I know, I know. I kept thinking you'd just leave a message. I-I haven't been up to it…"

"Oh, no! It's against our policy to leave messages. Frank always says this type of news shouldn't be delivered after a beep. He kept telling me he knew you would answer when you were ready."

Bless Frank Ballard and his stubborn wisdom.

"Well, I guess I am."

"I'm sorry?"

"I guess I'm ready."

"Oh. Oh! Well, then. This is just a courtesy call to let you know Corrie's tombstone is ready. You are welcome to pick it up yourself, but Frank usually delivers and installs them himself. We just need your permission, and we will take care of all the details and let you know when the job is complete. I can leave a message for that."

"That's fine," she said, weakly. "Just give me a call when it's done."

"Yes, of course, thank you, Mrs.…."

She hung up the phone and stared out the window, startling as the screen door slammed behind her. She turned in time to see Anna grab Caleb's baseball cap from his head with a giggle, Caleb whirl around and grab her by the waist, sweeping her off her feet in one twirling motion, their laughter filling a space inside of her she never knew was there.

"Hush, you two!" she scolded. "I just put the baby down."

"Oh!" Anna said, covering her mouth, tiptoeing over to the window where the bassinet lulled. Caleb followed and she watched as the two young parents kneeled together and gazed down at their son, mesmerized. A soft silence nudged into that space inside recently carved out by laughter. She floated over to Caleb and Anna and joined them in the reverie.

Rowan's long lashes crested the swell of his cherubic cheeks, his perfectly rounded head dusted with strawberry. She reached down to stroke his cheek and he made a small sucking motion with his lips in response. Anna placed her palm on his belly and their eyes met over the bassinet.

Oh, Corrie. If only you could see this little one. I couldn't love him more if he was my own flesh and blood.

Anna smiled and motioned for them to follow her to the screened porch, grabbing the baby monitor on the way. She sat down in the Adirondack chair and Anna and Caleb flopped onto the wicker loveseat. Anna leaned her head back on the plush pillows. She waited.

"Well? How did it go?"

Anna continued studying the ceiling fan. "I thought you might like to know," she drawled, "That you are now talking to Doctor Anna Ferris." She leveled her eyes and grinned.

"Oh, Anna! That's wonderful news! Congratulations!" They jumped up at the same time and she wrapped Anna in a happy hug. "How was it?" she asked, squeezing her young friend tight.

"It wasn't too bad. After an hour and a half of grueling questions," she rolled her eyes, "the committee said they were 'pleased to accept' my dissertation."

Caleb grinned. "But that's not all. Tell her the other news, Dr. Ferris."

"Welllllll," her grin was as big as the Cheshire cat's, as she backed up to arm's length. "They want me to continue my research." She paused for effect. "As a full time faculty member and Director of the university's new conservatory!" Anna's voice morphed into a squeal of delight, and she jumped up and down and, as they still had arms linked, they both bounced along in a little jumpy circle dance.

"Oh, Anna! It seems almost too good to be true. It's perfect for you. I'm so, so happy for you!"

Anna collapsed back down beside Caleb on the love seat. "I haven't told them yes yet."

"Why on earth not?"

Anna looked at the baby monitor sitting on the wicker coffee table in front of her. "I don't know if I can leave Rowan. I have to look into what kind of daycare is available and all that involves…"

"Daycare? Absolutely not. Our little man will stay with

me. At least for a while."

Anna stared. "You couldn't…I couldn't ask you to…"

"Nonsense. Nothing would make me happier."

Anna still looked dumbstruck. "I-I could pay you…"

"*We* could pay you," Caleb interjected, squeezing Anna's hand.

"And it wouldn't be every day," Anna said. "Just when I must teach and have office hours. Rowan could come with me to the greenhouse, and I could…"

"We will figure it out. But you mustn't let this opportunity pass you by. I can see how much it means to you."

Anna's eyes were glistening. "Thank you," she whispered, tears spilling. "I don't know what I would do without you. I am," she glanced at the baby monitor, "we are…so lucky to have you in our lives."

She glanced down at the plain gold band on the fourth finger of her left hand. "I am the lucky one," she said. And she meant it.

~

There was a chill in the air the morning the monument company called. She let it go to voice mail, just as she knew she would. But she played the message back immediately, unable to help herself. It was old Frank himself what called. His gruff voice filled her ear.

"Hey, there, this is Frank Ballard. I just wanted to let you know we got Corrie's tombstone all set up. It looks real nice, I think. I was hoping you'd do me a favor and let Sarah know…"

There was a pause, then he continued, a little catch in his voice.

"I know it's not…what any of us wanted, but…well, I think Corrie would like it. And if you're ever needing anything, I hope you'll let me know. Let me know if you don't like the way the stone turned out. And I'll be…well, you know where to find me."

The old man's care touched her. In her own grief, she'd almost forgotten about how Corrie's death was mourned by others. By the entire community, really. Frank and Corrie—those two were thick as thieves. As unlikely a pair as you'd ever see, but they got on. Both in love with the bees.

The least she could do is go see it so she could thank Frank properly.

She put on the kettle.

She had to do this right. She found the tin with Corrie's favorite blend and pulled it from the cupboard. She pried the lid loose and lifted the tin to her nose. The earthy scent of turmeric, mingled with ginger, black pepper, and cinnamon tickled her nose. She knew Sonja from the Apothecary Tea Room downtown made this blend with bee pollen, just for Corrie. She fixed her pot with the infuser and carefully measured out the tea and waited for the water to boil. When the whistle blew, she poured the water over the leaves and left them to steep.

She found her favorite loose tunic dress in the back of the closet and pulled on some blue jean leggings underneath. In the bathroom, she brushed her long hair until it shone, leaving it loose against her shoulders. She peered in the mirror and dabbed some concealer under her eyes. Her face had filled out these past few weeks. All those catering gigs—someone had to test the final recipes. She hesitated for a second and then opened the vanity drawer, pulled out a tube of rosy pink lipstick and traced her mouth. She looked in the mirror again and felt a sharp pang in her heart. For a moment she almost believed she was getting ready to meet Corrie.

Well? Wasn't she? She squared her shoulders and went back into the kitchen to pour the tea into a thermos. She placed the thermos in her market basket, along with some good dark chocolate and two paper cups.

She grabbed her straw hat on the way out and plunked it on her head. *Let's do this in style,* she thought.

~

The stone was as lovely a thing as such a thing could be. Frank had engraved a bee in the top right corner of the monument. She spread out the picnic blanket on the fine, new grass in front of the face of the stone and sat down, drawing her knees up to her chest and pondering. Someone had already planted a climbing rose on the partially shaded side of the gravesite. Sarah? Or Frank? She shook her head in wonder. She poured two steaming cups of the bee-pollen tea and set one down at the base of the gravestone. The other she cupped in her hands. The warmth of it felt good on her bare fingers, soothed the lump in her throat. She unwrapped the chocolate bar and broke it in two, placing half with the cup of tea at the stone's base.

She nibbled on her chocolate quietly. A chickadee gave a

soft whistly song in a nearby tree. *Hey, sweetie,* he said. *Hey, sweetie.*

She set the chocolate down on the blanket.

"Hey, sweetie," she said, softly. She took a sip of tea. "I'm sorry…I'm sorry it's taken me so long to come by." She swallowed and turned her face away from Corrie's name on the stone. "So much has happened. There's so much I want to tell you." She turned back to the stone. "I have this amazing little family in my life now. Anna and Rowan and Caleb…Somehow, I know you already know. You brought them to me. Those bees of yours…"

She swallowed again, eyes watering.

"Oh, Corrie. You would love them so much. Shoot, you already loved Caleb Brown. But Rowan…I've never felt the kind of love I feel for that child. Every time I look at him, I feel my heart will explode."

She talked to Corrie for an hour, letting tears and laughter spill over her words until she was wrung out, empty. She sat quietly for a while longer, sipping her lukewarm tea, letting chocolate melt on her tongue. Finally, she stood up and touched the stone. She traced her finger over the name engraved in the center.

Corinthia Mae Brooks

"Corrie"

Beloved wife and mother

"I love you, Corinthia Mae," she whispered.

20

She walked around to the back of the stone, trailing her hand along the smooth marble. She was surprised to see an inscription.

Tell the bees

She leaned in to read the small print beneath the inscription. *John Greenleaf Whittier,* it said. *What in the world?* Puzzled, she pulled out her phone and did a quick search for the man's name.

It was a poem. A long one. She sat down to read it.

Telling the Bees

Here is the place; right over the hill
   Runs the path I took;
You can see the gap in the old wall still,
   And the stepping-stones in the shallow brook.

There is the house, with the gate red-barred,
   And the poplars tall;
And the barn's brown length, and the cattle-yard,
   And the white horns tossing above the wall.

There are the beehives ranged in the sun;
   And down by the brink

Of the brook are her poor flowers, weed-o'errun,
Pansy and daffodil, rose and pink.

A year has gone, as the tortoise goes,
Heavy and slow;
And the same rose blows, and the same sun glows,
And the same brook sings of a year ago.

There's the same sweet clover-smell in the breeze;
And the June sun warm
Tangles his wings of fire in the trees,
Setting, as then, over Fernside farm.

I mind me how with a lover's care
From my Sunday coat
I brushed off the burrs, and smoothed my hair,
And cooled at the brookside my brow and throat.

Since we parted, a month had passed,—
To love, a year;
Down through the beeches I looked at last
On the little red gate and the well-sweep near.

I can see it all now,—the slantwise rain
Of light through the leaves,
The sundown's blaze on her window-pane,
The bloom of her roses under the eaves.

Just the same as a month before,—
The house and the trees,

The barn's brown gable, the vine by the door,—
Nothing changed but the hives of bees.

Before them, under the garden wall,
Forward and back,
Went drearily singing the chore-girl small,
Draping each hive with a shred of black.

Trembling, I listened: the summer sun
Had the chill of snow;
For I knew she was telling the bees of one
Gone on the journey we all must go!

Then I said to myself, "My Mary weeps
For the dead to-day:
Haply her blind old grandsire sleeps
The fret and the pain of his age away."

But her dog whined low; on the doorway sill,
With his cane to his chin,
The old man sat; and the chore-girl still
Sung to the bees stealing out and in.

And the song she was singing ever since
In my ear sounds on:—
"Stay at home, pretty bees, fly not hence!
Mistress Mary is dead and gone!"

—John Greenleaf Whittier, 1858

When she finished reading, she knew what she had to do.

~

She loaded her wheelbarrow with everything she'd need. The bolts of black tulle were too awkward to carry down the hill by herself. There were also fancy black ribbons to complete the outfit, scissors, tape, and thumb tacks.

When she arrived at her destination, she entered the shed and slowly donned the bee suit. She felt like an astronaut, so attired, and as she made her way to the hives imagined herself hopping across the surface of the moon—entering a place as strange as outer space.

Deftly and carefully, she wrapped each hive in the black tulle, taking care not to block the doorways. She worked as quickly as she could so as not to disturb her tenants. After wrapping all eight hives in tulle, she moved back to the first boxes and attached a fancy bow on the top frame with a thumb tack. Moving down the line, she did the same with the other seven hives.

When finished, she stepped back to admire her handiwork. A few forager bees crawled along the tulle, exploring this new addition to their home.

"What do you think, Love?" She asked the air. "Not too bad, huh?"

She looked up at the sky, pooling cloudless above her. Then turned to head back over to the shed.

You'll have to tell the bees.

She heard Corrie's voice in the shell of her ear. She hesitated.

"Now?"

Yes, my love.

"I'm sorry it's taken me so long, heart of my heart," she replied.

She smiled wryly and tried to recall the requirements:

The lyrics must rhyme.

They must be sung.

Each hive must be told individually.

For the first seven hives, she used the traditional rhyme she had found in one of Corrie's beekeeping books. She approached the first hive hesitantly, lingering in the shadows feeling foolish. Finally, she took a deep breath, stepped forward and tapped once on the hive. She let her hand rest on the frame and sang softly,

> "Bees, bees awake!
> Your master is dead and
> Another you must take!"

A few of the bees crawled on the thick glove and sleeve of her suit, curious. She watched them explore, all golden remnants of sunlight.

"I'm sorry," she whispered. "Corrie is gone."

She moved to the next hive, repeating the ritual. Knock once. Say the rhyme in that sing-songy voice. Give the bees time to hear.

At the final hive she knocked once, then closed her eyes—trying to remember the tune. The words would come, just as they always did for Corrie. Softly, to the tune of "She's Always a Woman to Me," she sang,

"The world is frequently kind and suddenly cruel
It gives love and takes it and makes you a fool
And so I must tell you your master is gone
You must say goodbye and continue the song.
…Mmm-mmm, mmm-mmm
Mmm-mmm, mmm-mmm-mmm-mmm."

She continued the humming, rubbing the side of the hive, watching the bees stir, circling, landing on her arm.

"Corrie is gone, little brownies. Corrie is gone."

She let the tears slide silently down her cheeks.

~

Back up at the house, she took her phone out on the porch swing to make the call. The sun was sinking behind the surrounding hills and she could hear the beginnings of the cricket castanet. She watched a honeybee dip into the orange flowers on the trumpet vine that trailed along the porch lattice. With a deep exhale she opened the phone and slowly dialed the now familiar number. One ring, two. After five rings the recorded message came on.

"Hi, Rhoda? I've made a decision about the bees…"

THE END

Also from T. S. Poetry Press

Waiting for Neruda's Memoirs

by Laura Boggess

a novella in The Poetry Club Series